KID 8

By Linden Dalecki

AN IMPRINT OF HOUGHTON MIFFLIN COMPANY
BOSTON 2006

For information about permission to reproduce selections from this book, write to
Permissions, Houghton Mifflin Company, 215 Park Avenue South, New York, New
York 10003.

www.houghtonmifflinbooks.com

The text of this book is set in Filosofia.

Library of Congress Cataloging-in-Publication Data

Dalecki, Linden.
Kid B / by Linden Dalecki.
p. cm.
Summary: Barely making it through high school,
Breslin—known as Kid B—longs to escape from Beaumont, Texas,
and pursue his talents as a break dancer.
ISBN-13: 978-0-618-60566-8 (pbk. : alk. paper)
ISBN-10: 0-618-60566-5 (pbk. : alk. paper)
[1. Break dancing—Fiction. 2. Conduct of life—Fiction. 3.
Family problems—Fiction. 4. Dance—Fiction.] I. Title.
PZ7.D152613Kid 2006
[Fic]—dc22
2005038069

ISBN-13: 978-618-60566-8

Manufactured in the United States of America

HAD 10 9 8 7 6 5 4 3 2 1

FOR JOSH

A-side
On the Grind

The B-Boys of Beaumont

The business ward had lots of tall buildings but they were all kind of old and crumbling. And before we could even make it to the spot downtown a hard rain was hitting the city. Rain was a good thing that summer 'cause it helped to keep things cool. It was me and Trick T leading and Big Vance following behind, like he usually does.

Vance is big like his name says and none too fast, but he's got power and always got a few crazy moves up his sleeve. Trick is a natural b-boy, straight up, no two ways about it. Breaking didn't come natural to me like it did to Trick. I had to work hard for every move 'cept maybe backspinning and the worm, but they're so ol' skool and simple nobody can really count them as moves these days.

When we passed by Kyle's Five and Dime the rain was

still coming but the sky was starting to look like the sun might peek out. On one side of Kyle's you could still see the Krush Krew tag put up by Ruina like two years back when we first crewed up. KRUSH KREW FOR LIFE is what the yellow tag read, but Ruina's style was so his that even heads couldn't hardly read it, let alone the regular people in the city. But even if the tag said what it did, Ruina was out in Cali on a trick-bike sponsorship. Couldn't hardly even get him on the phone anymore.

So instead of the old four-man Krush Krew it was down to me, Trick, and Vance. The plan was to get set up outside the Jefferson Theater and put on a show. Most everybody would stop and sneak a look, even the old business guys. If some people felt like putting some change on the sidewalk we never stopped them, but that's not how the police saw things. And if it wasn't panhandling, they could get us for disturbing the peace, even if Vance never pushed the box past five on the volume dial. The rain had come to a drizzle, so Vance took the garbage bag off and set the box on the ground. Vance always talked too loud, even when he was being nice.

Vance scoped me and Trick and was like, "Y'all down?"

Trick was all, "Why you gotta ask?"

That was just like the two of them, since Vance was

Mr. Polite unless you pushed him to the wall. Then you had to watch out, 'cause you couldn't guess what Vance might do if things got hyped. With Trick it was almost just the opposite. When things were chill, Trick would try and speed things up. But when things got hyped he'd keep cool under the stress. I guess it all kind of balanced out somewhere.

Vance pressed play on the box. A dirty beat kicked in, and Trick hit the deck. Right away everyone who was walking by came to a stop. Me, I like to uprock a little before I hit the ground, but not Trick. He always gets right into it. He threaded around like a pretzel and then busted out a vertical pushup, and you could hear the people in the crowd breathe in together all at once.

Trick's legs slashed around and almost hit some gray-haired guy wearing a suit, but Trick never hit anything or anyone unless he meant to. Most the crowd sort of laughed and the old guy walked away quick, like he was steamed about it, even though Trick was just having a good time and not trying to make anyone feel bad.

Trick got up and was like, "Hit it, Kid."

But I figured Vance was the one who'd brought the box, so I motioned for him to go next. Big V got into some crazy locking and popping. What Vance didn't have in style and timing he always made up for in power and letting it all hang loose. And when it came down to it, going all out and acting the fool was almost as good as being in full control. Plus, it always cracked people up. Vance did some of his jelly-belly rolls and had me and everybody laughing so hard that by the time he was done and I was up, I was almost out of breath.

I did my best to concentrate and get my head clear so I could put my focus on what I was doing. As soon as I got into some uprock I could feel that good feeling take over, and pretty soon it was only moves and colors and the beat. I dropped and busted out a coffee grinder, then flipped over for a few crickets. The crowd was eating it up like it was peach ice cream, which it really wasn't. But the adrenaline kicked in even more and made me try for a windmill.

I tried, but didn't get much past my left shoulder before I landed flat on my back. Not even one rotation, let alone a windmill that really spins. I threw out a freeze to make the crowd think I had tried to land flat on my back like that, but I probably only fooled maybe half the people watching, if that.

Before I could even stand I saw Vance reach for the box and shout, "Police!" I don't even remember getting up, just me and Trick and Vance running down Fannin Street and ducking into a tiny little alley. The police car couldn't even squeeze into it.

The police guy riding shotgun rolled down his window and shouted, "Go back where you came from."

Nobody got out of the car, so 'bout halfway down the alley we stopped running. I figured most police don't like it when they see us kind of kids having a better time than they probably ever had.

We knew how things were. And whenever we went to break downtown, we never parked our bikes near the dance spot. When we walked back past Kyle's Five and Dime the sun looked about ready to set. It made the yellow KRUSH KREW FOR LIFE tag glow orange. FOR LIFE . . . Yeah, right—then where was Ru? It hit me just then that words and names don't always mean what they say they do, even if people meant them when they used them. And how just like me and Trick and Big Vance had nicknames, so did the area around Beaumont. They started calling it Spindle-top like a hundred years ago when they went digging for oil and it came shooting up so high and strong out of the ground they couldn't stop it.

By the time we got rolling on our bikes the sun was hitting the water. And even all the oil refineries, train yards, broken-down mills, and rusted-out factories had a natural glow to them. Times like that made Beaumont seem pretty. And I remembered some substitute teacher who told the class that "Beaumont" stood for "pretty" in Cajun. My guess was that whoever the Cajun was that named Beaumont must have been looking at a sunset, about like the one me and Trick and Vance were looking at. And I tried to imagine how things might have looked if they never dug so deep into the ground that it changed the name of the place.

BREAKBEAT 1
INTRO TO ALGEBRA

When I rolled up to Jefferson High that morning the sun was so strong I could feel it burn my neck. Not that good warm feeling like when you jump out from cold water and the sun hits you. More like when you feel solar radiation and not just the heat going direct into your skin. Jefferson still had those green and white helium balloons tied to the front roof. And some big ol' green-on-white banner that said WELCOME TO SUMMER SCHOOL, DUMB-DUMB. Some prankster had tagged the red comma and the word *dumb-dumb* onto the banner. It was a okay joke, even if it was partly on me.

I locked my bike to a rusty old NO LOITERING AT ANY TIME signpost. I sometimes forgot my lock combo, but I had it written on my bedroom wall and usually kept a copy in my secret jeans pocket just in case. One bad thing 'bout summer school was Trick and Vance had already passed Intro to Algebra back in spring, not like they was science geeks or something. So I was the only one who had to be there.

While I handled my business I wondered about how come all school bathrooms I ever been in are exactly the same. Same type stalls, same tiles, same mirrors. Kind of like the same guy built all school bathrooms everywhere. I wondered if it was just schools in East Texas or if it was the same even in cool places. I guess Katrina-ville is cool and my real moms had took me and my brother Earl there by train once, back when she was alive. But I wondered about places I'd never been to. Places like New York and Cali. Maybe I'd call Ruina and ask about the school bathrooms there. But like I said, he wasn't returning calls lately. I had one of them shiny extreme sports mags, and in the middle was a pic of Ru doing a flip on his bike in some competition in Cali. The words under the pic said, "Second Place Winner. Ruina Stovall. Beaumont, Texas." Another pic on the same page showed Ru with a hot *chica* on both sides of him. Mane. That boy was made and paid.

I heard the main door to the bathroom open. Wes

coughed three times and I knew it was cool to come out of the stall. Before I opened the stall door I heard Wes whisper back and forth to somebody 'bout something. But I couldn't make out the words. I opened the door and scoped Wes's freshman sidekick, Latrell. He stuffed something into the front of his jeans. It was a mean-looking snub-nosed pistol with a red-taped handle. And it was real. Wes rammed Latrell back so hard against the bathroom mirror it busted. It near sounded like a car crash and made a hella mess. Wes got in Latrell's grill. "How many times I gotta tell you not to pack at schoolio, foolio? Meet me at Zero's. Now get lost."

Latrell nodded to Wes and hustled on out of there real quick-like. Wes turned and scoped me up and down. "You didn't see that gat."

I figured it was best to play along. I put my hands up. "What gat?"

Wes grinned, flossin' his gold tooth with the princess-cut rock. Then he wiggled a bottle of lemon-lime soda muddied up with purple stuff.

"Five green ones, Kid."

I told him, "Yo, it's mixed with soda, dog, not Courvoisier." I motioned to my new yellow Chucks. I'd painted them Vogue yellow myself. Vogue yellow's the same color yellow as the stripe you see on the side of Vogue tires. Ru used to bomb all our sneaks before he left for Cali. "Plus, I just got these."

Wes was all, "Shyeah, they nice . . ."

Lots of us around this part of Texas say "shyeah" or "jyeah" when we want to say "yeah" 'cept stronger. Kind of like putting chicory in your coffee to punch it up, which is something else the peeps around here are all about.

But Wes wasn't going for it. "I ain't a grocer—I'm a pharmacist. You come to me to get your lean on, huh? I'm popping cancer patient hydro-pro seals. Somebody gotta pay the supply chain all the way to *Nuevo L.* Not to mention bonehead Latrell. You can't respect how I flip, sip soda or sip this . . ." He grabbed his pickle with his left hand.

I slapped a five into his right hand and told him, "I ain't got a microscope and tweezers."

Wes gave the bottle over and walked out. I went back in the stall and drank down the whole bottle right quick so I could make class on time. Just when I finished the last bit, Latrell popped his head back in the bathroom and whispered, "Johnson coming."

Wes went loco on Latrell. "What'd I tell you 'bout getting lost?"

By then all I had was a soda bottle and far as I cared Johnson could bite mine. Johnson was a mean hall monitor. We called him Cookie Cop since that's how he was. He tried to bust me and everyone else he thought was doing liquid bars. But he was old and always a step behind the game.

During school year I always sat in back of the class, and repeating Intro to Algebra was no diff. Mr. Kaprinski seemed like a good teacher and like a pretty nice guy too. Not all the teachers at Jefferson were nice like that and cared. But I never could concentrate on numbers and stuff too good. With the liquid bar kicking in I was in my own zone, getting my lean on, and just about sleeping. But I saw something that kind of snapped me out of it.

Yeah, it was Alicia. She didn't smile but she gave me that look girls give you when they want you to know they want you to step to them. I squinted my eyes at her hair and even though it was dark black it shined that way bright things do when you squint. I figured maybe I was staring at her too long, and thinking that made me shift around in my seat. Plus, her right-hand girl, Teresa, gave Alicia a look. Like she got her panties in a bunch 'cause me and Leesha were checking each other.

The first time I ever seen Alicia was more than two years back at her *quinceañera*, which is like a girl's sweet fifteen mega b-day party. She was fine even back then but looked way more fine now that she was seventeen. Alicia's Uncle Timas paid everybody from Krush Krew and Magno Clique to put on a b-boy show at her *quinceañera*. I couldn't believe we got paid, 'cause that was before the Krew or the Clique had major skills, or major plex. Back then Peanut, who I'll tell you all about in a minute, was like Alicia's puppy-love boyfriend. Now she didn't even talk to him no more. I mean, she didn't even look at him or say hi. I scoped the front of the class, and Mr. Kaprinski kept babbling on about algebra: " . . . so, whenever a problem can be simplified, simplify it. Take it from a pro, folks. This will make your job a whole lot easier. Break into groups of two or three and work the problem out . . ."

Some of the class listened to Mr. K, but most of us just used it as a chance to chatter and chill. When I scoped Alicia again she smiled at me real direct-like. I heard a little snigger and figured it was Warren or Peanut, player-hating on me. But I'm not really any kind of player, and Alicia just smiled at me one time. Warren was a tall dark brother. Peanut was a skinny Tejano who mostly let Warren settle on what to do. But sometimes Peanut got way out of control, so you had to watch him.

Plus, he was still jonesing bigtime for Alicia and kept trying to hook it back up with her.

What you really gotta know is, Peanut and Warren were one-half of the Krush Krew's most worst enemy crew, the Magno Clique, which also had Izzle and Dap. Izzle and Dap were both already way out of high school and real old, like twanky-two or maybe even more old than that. Magno Clique was the only other posse in B-town that could represent as real b-boys. When it came to Krush Krew versus Magno Clique battles, it was pretty much me against Warren, Trick against Dap, Peanut against Big Vance, and Izzle against Ruina. 'Cause b-boys usually square off against the guy who's closest to them in skills and moves and whatnot.

Warren was sort of the leader of Magno Clique, even if Dap was their best dancer. And I think me and Trick were kind of like half chiefs, but we never really talked about it like that. Anyway, Warren had two sheets of paper on his desk. Both pieces had big ol' circles drawn smack dab in the middle. Him and Trick both wanted to be club DJs, but Warren was always fronting and acting like he was from Houston's Dirty Third. That was a lie, since he only lived there one school year with his auntie. Warren spun the papers, fronting like he was DJ Screw mixing with paper turntables. He made scratching noises from out his mouth, and it actually came out sounding not too bad.

Peanut bopped his head to the human beatbox scratch Warren was spitting, then busted out a rap with some Mexican words mixed into it. Peanut's family had moved to Beaumont from the Valley, just about the same time Ru's moms and him had come in from Arizona. Ru and Peanut could both talk and rap Mexican as good as American.

"*Pinche pendejo, remolino del pellejo*, a pink *zorrero* trying to get with Guerrero . . ."

I knew Alicia's last name was Guerrero, but other than that couldn't really pick up what Peanut was putting down. It came out sounding good anyway, maybe 'cause the liquid bar was in full effect. It made me bust out a few little popping moves right there in my seat.

"Punk-ass wigger best hail him a cab-o, 'cause only Peanut's butter mix with *al guayabo* . . ."

Soon as he rapped the word "wigger" I stopped my poplocking and tried to think up a good comeback. But the lean made my head work too slow. Mr. Kaprinski kept pointing to formulas on the board and rambling on, but I couldn't make sense of it: ". . . if you're stuck then clear the parentheses, okay? Then combine like terms by adding coefficients. See, this is fun. Now, combine the constants . . ." Man, who could keep up? I started to think how dumb it was for someone to be sipping syrup. It just made the hard stuff, like thinking up a good comeback, even harder.

I remembered how one time Dad called my real moms dumb and she fired right back at him, "I may be dumb, but I'm not stupid." She used to get really sad from time to time, but I missed her a lot and I know my brother Earl and my dad did too. But we didn't let it show. It was probably hardest on Dad since he knew her the longest. Plus, I think he thought me and Earl pretty much blamed him and maybe he was sort of right about that. My stepmom, Lori, did codeine and she could never throw down comebacks like my real moms used to. Warren leaned over to Peanut and made sure to talk loud enough so I could hear him too.

I shoulda knowed not to poplock in class, 'specially around Magno Cliquers. Poplocking's basically moving so it looks like a wave's going through you, or like you're some kind of robot instead of a regular person. Peanut kept up the same flow over Warren's beatbox but changed up his lyrics to mess with my head about Alicia.

"Yo, nut, you heard about that spastic junk they call touretic syndrome?"

Peanut was like, "Nah, mane, them's ballerina moves, mane. Ain't you heard how he took them ballerina lessons?"

Peanut's dis got a little chuckle out of Warren, and Peanut kept on. "That's why they call him Kid B. Stands for Kid Ballerina."

I bit my tongue and fronted like I didn't hear nothing. Warren jumped in with, "Heck, I thought it meant Kid Bee-otch." Then him and Peanut high-fived and busted up cackling.

I came back with a "Y'all so funny I forgot to laugh."

Warren was all, "White cracker's Paul Wall self thinks his lil' clique gonna hit the H-Town Throw Down, get scouted and sponsored. Psss, whatever."

None of it was true, 'cept the part about the Krew maybe wanting to represent at the H-Town Throw Down. Even though I'm a b-boy and not a MC, I still get called Paul Wall a bunch cause I'm Caucasian, which is how they call Anglo on them test forms they make you bubble in with a number-two pencil.

Anyway, Peanut had to chime in, "Ha. Can't no one but Magno Clique rep B-town, you feel me?"

I tried to sound chill. "Get off the gas, Peanut. Krush Krew's gonna put B-town on the radar. Remember I said it."

Peanut and Warren chuckled it up and high-fived. Warren and the rest of Magno Clique knew all about Ru not being around. Warren asked, "How's life in Cali for Ruina? He dogged y'all bigtime last year. He still got that bike sponsorship?"

"Ruina or no Ruina, I guarantee you Krush Krew gets props for B-town. Y'all should just stay home."

After I put that down, Warren squeaked out a loud and nasty fart. "Stop flossin'. My booty don't stank *half* as bad as y'all Krush Krew losers."

I flipped them the bird. They both cackled louder than before and Peanut bit my poplocking moves, 'cept made them look silly. Then he passed a poplock over to Warren, who also bit my style and tried to make it look juvenile.

Not to show out, but I knew they was both jealous of how Alicia was looking over at me before. Most 'specially Peanut. I tried hard, real hard, to play like I didn't hear nothing. But I felt my face turn red, so I knew they knew I heard everything. The lean was fading and I busted out on Warren with "Yeah? And y'all stank so bad

I heard Mr. Kaprinski's givin y'all A-pluses *not* to raise y'all's hands."

Warren didn't have anything to come back with, so Peanut covered for him. "Say what? Dang, Dubya."

I figured I already had them beat and was like, "You heard me, son."

Warren scoped Peanut and chuckled for a bit to give hisself more time to think something up. "Dang, P. We gotta take out the mamma trash." He turned, trying to look all serious. "Your mamma's so nasty I called her for phone sex and she gave me a ear infection." That got a giggle out of Peanut. But I had something to top it.

"Speaking of moms, I just got off yours. And she told me she's worried about all the sixty-nineing you and P been doing on each other."

Yeah, that pretty much did it. Warren got all jumpy in his seat. "Motha, we'll see who's fruity."

Peanut joined in with "Shyeah, we'll see. After class. We'll see who's got the dopest set and who gets wrecked, punk."

One thing it seemed Magno Clique didn't get is how b-boying's more about being down with your boys than it is about the sets you can pull off. Don't get me wrong. Moves and skills are super important. But it wouldn't mean nothing if your crew wasn't there to see you represent. And the biggest thing isn't what goes down in the cypher—you know, the circle where you throw down your dance moves. The biggest thing is your boys always got your back outside the cypher. No matter how bad the situation might be. Even if it means everybody gets beat down to a pulp to back you. Having backup like that makes you more confident in everything you do. Even when you know that you don't know as many things or got as much bling or whatever as suit people might.

On the low I pulled out my cell. Really it was my brother Earl's phone, but he had two. I figured he wouldn't miss the one I basically adopted and was looking after. I typed in "911, BACKUP, BEHIND SCHOOL, ASAP" and sent the message out to my boys. Ten minutes left till class was out. Plenty of time.

I tuned in and scoped Mr. Kaprinski. He was tall even though he was the kind of guy who slouched down a few inches. "Guess that does it for today. I'll let you go in just a sec. But before I do, are there any questions?" No one in the class put a hand up. Dang. I needed time for my boys to respond. Kaprinski was like, "Not all at once," and he laughed at his own gag. I raised a hand up. Kaprinski saw me. "Yes, Breslin there in back."

"Umm . . . I was gonna ask about them gerunds."

"Pardon?"

"You know, gerunds." I heard a few kids in the front row chuckling.

Mr. Kaprinski looked confused. "Do you mean the number trick?"

"Umm . . . gerunds. Yeah."

"Why don't you see me alone? The rest of you are free to go."

Dang. What'd I do now? The whole class chattered and pretty much everyone made for the door all at once. Alicia turned and gave me that look again. It was so strong it made my guts drop. But I kind of liked the feeling. Warren and Peanut stood in the doorway and flexed a little. Warren pulled out his cell, and both of them grinned at me when they strutted out the classroom. That made my guts drop in a diff way. A way I didn't like.

Mr. K shuffled the homework assignments around on his desk. I thought he was gonna call me on not handing mine in. I was about to come up with a excuse when he was like, "You do know what class you're in, Breslin. Yes?"

"Yeah. Intro to Algebra."

"Well, that's good. Well, you should also know that a gerund's an English term."

"I passed it, but I didn't do so good in that neither."

Mr. K lowered down his head and peeped over his glasses' rims at me. "Sounds like you've got a great future in store, Breslin."

I had to try and set him straight. "I'm good at things, like . . . like b-boying." But you could tell he didn't know what us b-boys did. "You know, breakdancing."

Mr. K shook his head and snapped his math book shut. "Yeah, sure. And if you can't make a living at it, then what? You end up unemployed with a cool hobby. Great. Just great."

Mean as he might of sounded, I rolled out of class figuring Mr. K didn't mean any harm by it. You know how lots of folks show you they care by riding you and whatnot.

BREAKBEAT 2
Backup Plus

Out in the hall I saw Alicia and Teresa going at it in Spanish. Leesha scoped my face. I don't know how, but she could tell I was bugging. And she asked me what was wrong.

I just told her, *"Hasta mañana."* I waved and rolled off quick 'cause I had the Warren and Peanut thing to deal with out in back of the school. I saw Johnson giving one of the janitors a hard time about the floor polish. I snuck down a side hall before he spotted me. I peeked out a dirty window to the back courtyard and saw Warren in his Windbreaker by hisself, pissing. He aimed his pee at a handrail. Then Peanut hoofed around the corner all in a huff.

Warren zipped up, then got all bowed up. He raised

his chin and made a ugly face like he thought he was a heavyweight boxer or somebody. Real slow-like, I opened the back door and rolled outside. That put a new look on both their faces. Then they played like they wasn't surprised. Even though I knew diff. And they both gave me a grin like they wasn't scared. Even though I seen right through that too.

Peanut was all excited, even started bouncing up and down. I don't think he'd have been so hyped if he was gonna go first. But he knew as good as me Warren wouldn't have that. Like I told you, Warren was pretty much bull goose of Magno Clique. He yanked off his Windbreaker and chucked it to the ground. He stared right at me. "Come and taste it. One on one, come and get some."

Still jumping up and down, Peanut accidentally bumped Warren. He pushed Peanut back against the peed-on handrail and told him to hang back.

Peanut checked in back his pants and saw a wet line. "Dang, dog! You got your pee on me."

I spit on the ground and stared at Warren. He was able to hold my stare. I picked at my nose like I was bored, even though I was edged out wondering why it was taking so long for the Krew to show.

Warren blinked. "This ain't a booger fight. I'ma make that nose bleed. Keep picking that snout, I'ma break it."

I held my stare on Warren and flicked a booger off my finger past Warren's face. Peanut chimed in, "Watch out! He probably got AIDS."

I walked up to Warren all slow and he stood his ground. Then he busted into some uprock. Some people call uprock "toprock." It's basically just the footwork you do before you drop and get into your groundwork and power moves. Warren got into his uprock, and his face came real close to hitting mine twice. But I didn't even blink once. I could tell that drove him a little loco.

Then it was my chance to uprock, and I got all up in Warren's grill with it. Next I hit the deck and did a bunch of tictacs, which some folks call Russian kicks. You hit the ground, lean back onto your hands, and slam your legs back till they hit your chest and shoulders. When your legs spring forward again you can even get your hands to lift off the deck and get air.

Warren came at me with some six-step, then hit three vertical pushups. His perfection. A b-boy's perfection is his best move. The one he uses to try and take the competition out. Six-step's a downrock step, so you're on your hands and feet dancing in a circle on the floor. Sometimes face-up, sometimes face-down. Vertical pushups are like they sound. You push up from the ground on your hands, with your feet pointing straight up. On his third vertical pushup Warren kind of wobbled and fell back. He caught his balance and acted like he was all still in control.

Warren asked, "What else you got?" You could hear he was pretty much out of breath.

I airwalked all around Warren, which is when you glide over the ground in all directions to where it looks like you're floating. Sort of like ol'-skool moonwalking but all over the place, not just backwards. Not to floss, but it looks way more tight and stylin' than what Michael Jackson used to do. After being in Warren's grill, I air-walked over to Peanut and dissed him with a "How you like that, P.B. and J.?" Trick T had called him that once, and it got him even more loco this time around.

Peanut dropped to the deck for some six-step, did two circles, then started rubberbanding like a mug. Rubberbanding's where you start laid out on your back, spring up on your feet without using your hands. Then fall to your back again and keep doing the whole thing over and over. Pretty much any b-boy can kip up, which is springing up just one time from your back to your feet. But rubberbanding's hard as all get out.

On his last kip-up, Peanut landed on his feet, shouted "Shyeah!" in my grill, and pushed me back. It wasn't a friendly push neither. He pushed me so hard my booty landed a gang of feet from where I was standing.

Before I could even stand up, Peanut was all, "Paul Wall wannabe ass wigger." I tried to get up in his grill. But Warren stepped in the middle, so I was like, "You wanna mash, we can mash."

Warren scoped my fresh-out-the-box Chucks. He lifted his right foot real slow-like and grinded the muddy heel of his shoe on top of my left one. That was it. I shoved him back, hard. Warren jumped back right quick and came at me with a left hook. He connected pretty good with the side of my face.

The punch sent me back but I didn't fall. Warren grinned. Peanut jumped up and down. "You feel that, punk?"

In tackle mode, I made a dive for Warren's knees and got my arms around them. Warren put down a mess of punches and slaps on my head and face. But none of it hurt too bad. I could see Peanut's feet jumping up and down higher and higher. "Beat him down. Beat that white donkey."

What I did next isn't much to be proud of, but it saved

me anyway. I bit down on the side of Warren's left leg. And I mean real, real hard. "Motha fu . . ." was all I heard before I saw Warren bend down. He grabbed the side of his leg and I stood up.

Warren was near crying. "He bit me. The motha done bit me." He stayed doubled over. I chucked a uppercut to his face and he wobbled back, onto his behind. Without me even knowing, Peanut jumped in. He put a hard right to the back of my head. That sent me forward and I landed on Warren. From below, Warren wrestled and punched me as best he could. Peanut piled on with a knee to my lower back.

You don't need to guess how bad that whole mess hurt. "Aaahhh . . ." It almost sounded like someone else was yelling, but it was me. Even with my face on the deck I could see the two pairs of legs pumping out circles on bike pedals. And I knew I was pretty much safe and sound. Trick T and Big Vance both had on b-boy gear, so they must have been practicing when I 911'd them.

Trick T yelled out, "Yo, what's the deal?," which got Warren and Peanut's attention right quick. They scrambled to get up but Trick jumped his skin-and-bones self off his bike, straight onto Warren. And like a swolled-up white elephant, Big Vance jumped poor lil' ol' Peanut.

I stood up slow, ready to enjoy the show. I rubbed the dirt off myself and watched Trick scrap on the ground with Warren. Then they both popped up and went at it blow for blow. I turned and saw Big Vance wrestle his whole upper body onto Peanut, and I almost felt bad. Peanut's face got redder and redder and he couldn't really talk anymore. "I can't . . . I can't brea . . ." Vance lifted his torso for a second. Peanut gulped air and Vance got him in a full nelson.

Vance pile-drived Peanut's face into the dirt. A lot of times. You could see Vance's eyes bulge. He kept jacking Peanut's face up, then down, on each of his words. "You give? You give? Say uncle. Uncle! Speak up, gaywad. I can't hear you."

You could see Peanut was gonna pass out. I jumped behind Big Vance and tried to yank him off. "S'all good, Vance. It's cool." But he didn't even notice me. On Vance's next thrust, Peanut went limp. But Vance kept driving him into the dirt and I kept trying to snap him out of it. "Yo, it's copacetic, mane. You done knocked him out, partner."

I yelled to Trick, and him and Warren both looked. They stopped their scrapping and ran over. It took all three of us to yank Big Vance off Peanut's rag-doll self.

You could see Vance's body tense up, relax. Then tense up again. At the same beat he'd been slamming Peanut.

Warren leaned over Peanut. In looks, Warren could have been Trick's cousin, since they're both skinny and tall. But Trick's dark black, and Warren's got freckles and that redbone color to him. Even his hair's brick red too. Warren shook P, but the boy was knocked out stone cold. Warren's eyes got big. "Peanut? Wake up, man. Yo, P?"

Just then, Izzle and Dap rolled into the school parking lot in Dap's El Camino lowrider. Dap pulled the El C right up to the edge of the lot. Like I told you, they were both real old, like twanky-two and twanky-three. Izzle always ran little errands and chores for Warren's cousin Branford, who slang sizzurp in the Magnolia section of town.

Dap's real name was Carlos Hidalgo, but he's Oriental, not Mexican. His daddy and moms came from straight out the Philippines, and his older sister, Eva, was even born there. Eva was way old, like maybe even thirty, but still double-dang hot. Dap worked three years at the same refinery as my brother, Earl. But he was canned for spending too much time in front of the mirror one morning and being late to his work detail one too many times. And Dap was late this time too. Even if he was stylin' in razor-creased jeans and a double-breasted jacket. Izzle stepped out the El Camino first, a ol'-skool gold dookie chain swinging on his neck. Then Dap got out. They took in the scene down by us. They scoped Peanut on the ground and ran our way.

Trick jumped on his bike and yelled, "Roll out! Come on, y'all!" I jumped right quick on the axle extenders of his back wheel. And Vance was already pedaling mad hard out in front of us. Trick got us moving. I turned and saw Izzle and Dap leaning over Peanut and talking to Warren. They hoofed it after us but it was too late. All they could do was picture us rolling.

Once we were safe and away from school I remembered my wheels. "Hold up. My bike's up in front the school."

Trick was all, "We can roll back later." Probably a good idea, since who knew if Warren, Izzle, and Dap might still be lying in wait for the Krew. After a hour or so, we cruised back and got my bike. All three of us had diff type trick bikes but painted them all Vogue yellow. We sometimes called it Krush Krew yellow 'cause we used it for all our tags and stuff. My bike was the cheapest, then Trick's, then Vance's. Vance's family wasn't really bling. But compared to mine and Trick's they was. Mainly 'cause his daddy was a foreman down at the refinery. I think he even bossed my brother, Earl, a few times.

Me and Trick hung back and let Vance stay out front. Trick scoped me like, "Is Vance loco?" Usually after a good scrap, after a fight we'd won, we'd all be amped. But this time was diff. None of us knew how bad Vance hurt Peanut. If Vance had just stopped pile-driving before he knocked him out, then we could of been celebrating. Instead, it was like we all had headaches trying not to stress about it.

Quiet enough that Vance couldn't hear I asked Trick, "You really think P's gonna be okay?"

"I ain't trying to think on it."

Vance slowed down so he was just in front of me and Trick. I asked real quiet in Trick's ear, "What if Vance killed him?"

Trick talked back to me real quiet. "Shut your syrup slot."

Vance slowed down and tried to listen in. So Trick changed the subject. "Y'all ready to mash the Magno Clique at the H-Town Throw Down?"

I had to keep it bona fide. "It's going down right soon."

The H-Town Throw Down was only one of the baddest-ass b-boy competitions in the whole nation. On the real, H-town, aka the 713 or the 281, and A-town, aka the 512, got some of the mega-tightest b-boy matches going down on the planet. Me and the Krew had been practicing moves on and off for over two years. But the H-Town Throw Down was hardcore. The real deal. Plus, we'd lost Ruina to that Mega-Bike sponsorship he signed on for just before last year's Throw Down. So the Krew wasn't able to represent.

Big Vance was back to his regular loud self. "Six weeks, fudge packer. We can still beat the drop."

I told him, "Nah, I was speaking for you."

Vance did a bike handplant. All the bucknasty flab on his white whale belly blobbed out. "Whooo! You scope that, players? My stylins should be on flow."

I told V to stop showing out and thought my next point was a good one. "School gym ain't open summer. We can't even push weight."

But Trick had other ideas. "Y'all need free weights, my daddy got free weights."

Vance asked, "Since when, simp?" before I could.

"Ever since he been in the brick business, swoll." Vance was chunky enough to be called swoll. And he mostly never took it personal if me or Trick was to rag him a little on it. But then he never thought it was too funny neither.

The picture of Peanut lying on the ground kept jumping into my head and made the back of my throat all dry. "I'm thirsty. Y'all wanna hit Krystal?" Krystal serves up a good burger and fries. But I was jonesing for a soda.

If I'd remembered what day of the week it was I could of told you Trick's answer before I heard it. "Nah, it's Wednesday. Gotta help the moms with grocery shopping."

And Vance was all, "Promised my little bro I'd whup his be-hind on Nintendo." Then he held out his right elbow, Krush Krew style. We all three knocked elbows together. Then forearms. Then fists. And we all three were like, "Krush Krew for Life." But none of us was really sure how long the Krew would last. Look at what happened with Ruina.

Vance pedaled off. I scoped Trick and had to go there. "Trick. You really think we ready to mash at the Throw Down nex month?"

Trick pedaled away and I followed after him. He talked more like he was trying to make hisself believe what he was putting down than to hype me. "Shyeah, I think we ready. Matter of fact I'm one hundred 'bout it, mane. We ready."

I was like, "Really? One hundred? I ain't so sure."

Trick was all, "Shyeah, one hundred. Ain't you heard

me the first time?" Then he shook his head. "Shit. I don't know. Maybe I ain't so sure neither, Kid. But maybe I gotta hear you are."

We pedaled down a side street, alongside the rail tracks. I asked, "Yo, Trick, what do we do 'bout Vance?"

Trick rolled his shoulders up. "Don't stress. First we wait and see what happened to Peanut."

"T. Could I ask you something?"

We swerved around a corner and Trick nodded. "Go on."

"You ever think about getting out of B-town? I mean, like, get out for good?"

Right after we banked the corner you could see a real pretty girl with long legs just kicking down the sidewalk all by herself. Guess I can't blame Trick for letting my question jump in one ear and out the other.

Trick was like, "Whoa, Nelly. Betcha a dollar to a dime that I mack that dame. Peep my honey love game, Kid."

I straddled my bike and clocked him throwing his mack down. Seemed like his game was strong, which was regular for Trick. He chunked me the deuce. You know, when you throw up a peace sign. "Peace out, Kid."

I watched him walk his bike down the block, still macking on the bopper. I figured maybe I'd said the wrong thing. That maybe I should have told Trick what he wanted to hear. And there was a small piece of me that hoped what he wanted to hear maybe wasn't even a lie. That maybe we really were good enough to hit the Throw Down and represent. My ears just barely made out a far-off freight train rumbling East real slow-like. It had a low and lonely tone that made me feel sad and good at one and the same time.

BREAKBEAT 3
EARL ACTS A STANKHOLE

I banked the corner onto my street and slowed before I got to our house. The outside of the house is shithouse green and always put some shame in my game. Not 'cause of the shithouse green but 'cause no one cared about it. No one tended to it. At least not since my moms died. Lori was my stepmom but I never thought of her like a real moms. She was always just around and I had to pretend like I respected her or Dad would get mad. Really, Dad didn't pay too much mind to me respecting her. Now it was more like Earl was the one who did.

Earl's my older brother by four years. Me and him used to be best friends like real brothers are supposed to be. But ever since he started working at the petroleum refinery over by Port Arthur he kind of became a stankhole. But that wasn't what I was thinking 'bout when I rolled up to the house that day. I was thinking 'bout the souped-up blue Iroc-Z across the street from our house. Some dude with dark watered-back hair got into it and shut the door. I rolled toward it slow on my bike. Whoever was in the slab must've saw me 'cause he rolled up his tinted windows before I could really scope who it was.

Then he peeled down the street like Schumacher or somebody and I gave chase. But even on Vance's Diamondback Viper there's no way I could of beat out a Camaro. The guy took the corner, skidded out, and fired a bullet at me. At least that's what I thought for a lickety-split second. Really it was just the engine backfiring once.

That was the last time I ever seen that slab. But I figured I knew what it was doing on my block. I slammed the door on my way in so Lori would know I knew. That's mainly how she and me talked anyways. By slamming doors and chucking stuff around. I went into the kitchen and flicked some of the old yellow paint off the wall. Sometimes I did that when I was stressed. You could see green paint underneath when you pulled the yellow flakes off. Purple was my real moms's favorite color, but she'd painted the kitchen yellow back when we moved in when I was three.

My stepmom, Lori, just sat there smoking with the

kitchen radio playing static with some pokey old country tune. It was already Wednesday but she was flipping through the Sunday comics like that's all she been doing all day. But I knew why that guy in the blue Camaro was out there, and it wasn't to read last Sunday's *Beaumont Enterprise*. I stole a real quick look at her tits. You could tell she didn't have no bra on under her dress. I mean, not like I really scoped them in that way or whatever. Behind the newspaper I peeped a glass of purple stuff she was trying to hide. And just like usual, Lori tried to switch things around and make me seem like the one who done something wrong.

"They let you out early?"

I pretended not to hear. I just opened the fridge and grabbed out a pitcher of red Kool-Aid. I filled me a glass and started to walk out. But she couldn't just let things be. "You playing hooky?"

I told her straight up, "You ain't my real moms."

"Thank God for small miracles."

"My real moms wasn't a ho." I got her with that one. Yeah. Her face got all twisted and stuff.

"Why you always got a bug up your behind when your daddy's driving?"

I swigged down half the glass. Lori took a big drag and blew it across the kitchen at me. I couldn't think up a comeback right off. So I stopped before I got to the living room, like that's what I'd planned to do. Then I guzzled down the rest of the glass. It gave me that fuzzy feeling in the throat that soda gives you when you drink it too fast. Which is funny since it wasn't soda.

"You hear me, Breslin?"

Dang. I shoulda just walked out the kitchen after I got her face twisted up. All I could think to say was "You ain't allowed to call me that." Lame. I know.

See, my moms gave me that name, Breslin. I think it was her great Paw Paw's name from way back when they came from Ireland or wherever. Then one of the Yardley twins gave me the nickname Kid B way back even before I can remember. They were identical and the two of them together was my best friend. Just before third grade they moved to some auntie's in Texarkana 'cause Mr. Yardley skipped town. The refinery wanted the authorities to bust him for juking three cans of high-gloss paint, but he just disappeared. Now Kid B's what everyone called me, 'cept sometimes old people like Mr. Bilcox and Mr. Kaprinski. But Lori knew she wasn't supposed to call me Breslin. She knew I hated to hear her say it. So then I put the attention on her. "Who was that guy?"

She got all quiet and ashed into her coffee saucer. "Who?" She was real good at playing stupid since she was pretty much there to begin with.

I was like, "Don't act dumb like that. I saw him, and I saw the blue Trans-Am or Camaro. Or whatever he was tippin'."

Then she really got into her act. "Well, maybe Mr. Detective better run a police check, 'cause I don't know what you're talking about."

I was like, "I'ma tell Dad. I'ma tell Earl when he gets back."

Lori stood up and the little black circles in her eyes got even smaller. She passed me by on her way to the living room. "Tell your drunk daddy whatever you want, you little prick."

I felt something strong inside me getting beat down and torn out. That's how Lori could make you feel when she burned you good like that. I heard her turn on that favorite soap opera she always watches and I poured myself another glass of Kool-Aid. I tried not to look at her when I passed through the living room to get to my room. Under my breath but loud enough for her to hear it I dropped, "And I know you sippin' codeine too . . ."

One thing you might notice 'bout us b-boys is we gotta have space where to break. My room wasn't big, but I always kept the center floor real clear of stuff. The corners of my room, that's another story. And you shoulda seen all the posters up on my walls. *Wild Style*, *Beat Street*, *Breakin'*, *Krush Groove*, Fred Astaire and Ginger Rogers in *Shall We Dance*, Paul Wall, Slim Thug, *Rize*, *The Warriors* (yeah, the original one), *The Harder They Come*, *Dragon Master Showcase*, *Tenjo Tenge*, *Saumurai Camploo*, Bruce Lee in *Enter the Dragon*, Mike Jones, *Stormbreaker*, UK International Breakdance Championship, *Breakin Away*, *Inside the Circle*, H-Town Throw Down XII, and the Nicholas Brothers in *Pie Pie Blackbird*. I could keep going, but that covers a mess of them.

You might be curious about a b-boy having a Bruce Lee poster. We not only groove on the types of kung fu moves he can put down, but also the concepts he has on them. I mean, in most his movies he talks about how you shouldn't put a beatdown on people just 'cause you can. And that's how b-boys are supposed to think. 'Specially since the first b-boy crews were basically gangs who stopped using knifes and guns to fight and started having dance battles to show who *could* have won if it was a real fight to the death. 'Cept in a dance battle no one gets hurt. And you can even bite a few dope moves from the competition to use against them in the next battle. The White House should of given them original b-boys a bunch of presidential fitness medals or whatever.

Anyway, with Lori being around, I made sure to lock

the door to my room. I put my cell on the dresser. Well, it was really Earl's but I told you how he had two and all. I popped a gray screwed and chopped tape in my boom box. See, the way we like our music here in Beaumont kind of came from what Robert Earl Davis Junior, aka DJ Screw, did in Smithville and Houston a long minute ago. Basically all our mixtapes get screwed down and chopped up. Even all the big-name stuff from whatever coast. I did my thirty afternoon pushups. I like to get my feet on my bed first cause it's harder and the only way to build up strength is to make it harder on yourself. The song was slow enough that I could do each pushup on the beat.

I switched in a up-tempo mixtape and busted out some footwork. I was really getting into my uprock when there was a loud knock. I figured it had to be Lori, come to mess with me 'bout something. I wiped the sweat off my forehead and asked what she wanted. But I heard Earl shouting, "Open the damn door!" I got up and opened it. I forgot to mention that Earl's three inches taller than me and maybe like forty pounds heavier. And most of that weight's not fat.

I acted all caj. "Huh?"

Earl muscled his way past and yanked the plug on my boom box. He saw the cell on my dresser. He grabbed it up and waved it in the air. "Mine."

I reminded him, "You got the company one."

"Yeah, and that's mine too. So don't be touching it. And don't be blowing Lori any bull. Got it?"

"I didn't—"

Earl wouldn't even let me finish. He was like, "All right?"

"But, I—"

He stepped toward me. "Okay? Y'understand?"

"But she . . . some yuppie dude was over here."

Earl swatted the back of my head for that one. Real hard too. "Who?"

I rubbed the spot where he hit me and told him, "I dunno who. In a blue Trans-Am, Camaro something."

Earl shook his head like he didn't believe me. "Yeah? And what'd he look like?"

"I dunno, I just saw . . ."

Earl stepped even closer, chest to chest. "You gotta stop lying. And I want you to apologize to Lori."

"I'm not lying, Earl. For real, dog."

"I'm not a dog, and you're not a coon, wannabe. So get off the gas."

Yeah, him saying that really got to me. So I didn't hold back neither. I showed him I knew the real deal. "You just take her side 'cause she gnaws your bent pickle."

That got to him bad and he boxed my right ear. It

dropped me to the floor. Just that one left hook of his. I thought he broke something in my head. I yelled when I saw him yank my UK poster off the wall. He tore it to shreds in two seconds. I squinted up. I saw him go for my *Beat Street* poster. And I mean the original one. "All right, all right, I'm sorry. Listen up. All right, Earl, I'm sorry. I'll tell her I'm sorry. C'mon, mane. Please."

Earl had his hands on it like he was gonna tear it up. But he just stood there grinning. Just enjoying that I was begging him not to make confetti of it along with the UK poster. He crumpled it and chucked it on the bed. When he left, I uncrumpled the *Beat Street* poster and collected up all the UK poster bits. I pieced them together on my bed as best I could. I made sure to set the volume low before I flipped the box on again. Then I got back into my footwork.

At dinner that night Lori made the only kind of mac and cheese she could. Runny. I just poked at it with my fork and watched some of the goo drip to the plastic red and white checkered tablecloth. I cut a burnt hot dog in half and forked it into my mouth. Lori glanced over at me and I made sure to grimace. Earl just kept shoveling the runny slop into his mouth. He grinned at Lori like a real idiot and was all, "Damn, I'm starvin'."

I gave a little chuckle. "You gotta be." Lori looked hurt for less than a second, so I felt good for less than a second.

Of course the Dookie of Earl had to jump in. "What was that?"

I tried to play it off. "Nothin'."

Earl played it like he was all mature. "Maybe you should be with me at the refinery all day. Maybe then you'd learn to appreciate a home-cooked."

I called his bull-hockey. "Shyeah, right. Like that got anything to do with it."

Earl's eyes got all shiny and he pointed at me with his knife. "You're gonna clean that fucking plate."

Lori patted Earl's left hand. She acted all surprised by Earl's little show. Even though I knew she expected it and really pretty much sparked it out of him. She fake wagged her finger at him. "Earl, we're at the dinner table, baby." As if she even gave a queef about Earl using the F word on me.

Earl lowered his voice. "Yeah, well, excuse my goddamn French." He stared at me. "And aren't you supposed to be telling Lori something?"

I scoped my plate and tried to say it, but I couldn't at first. When I could, it came out quiet. "Sorry." Then I said "bitch" under my breath to show the both of them I didn't really mean it.

"Huh? I didn't hear you."

Lori smiled that fake smile of hers. "Well, I heard him. Apology accepted, Breslin. Everybody makes mistakes."

I told her, "Yeah, 'specially my dad." Lori's fake-o smile changed to a actual frown. Under the table, Earl booted the hell out of my shins. "Owww. Dang." It really did hurt.

Earl was all, "You gonna whine like a infant, you can go to your crib right now."

I stood up and tried to look tough. But inside I felt like I was about to cry just like a infant like Earl had said. And when I talked, it hurt my throat. "Why can't you just . . . ? You never treat me like . . . You ain't a brother. And if you ever hit me again . . ." I held up my fist but Earl just grinned and called my bluff.

"Yeah? Then what? Pussy."

I turned to Lori. "And I hate you too. You ain't my moms."

I made for the front door and didn't look back.

"Where you think you're—" was all I heard Earl say before I yanked the door shut behind me.

I never went home that whole night. I circled around

a parking lot for a couple hours on my bike. All I could think about was Peanut lying on the ground not moving. Deep in the middle of the night, I rolled past some of the oil refineries. In the dark they throw off a crazy glow that's almost pretty if you're in the mood for it. Then I did bike tricks in a little park till I got dog tired. I lay on a park bench, put my arm through my bike frame so no one could steal it, and caught some z's. When I woke up it wasn't really light yet. But you could see the sky getting some pink in it. Some bum walked past, talking to his-self. I got on my bike and rode back toward my hood.

My eyes felt a little puffy from not enough sleep and all that stressing 'bout Peanut. But being up early felt good. I rode alongside the railroad tracks. And I was even able to balance both wheels on one of the rails and roll that way for a whole mess of yards. I saw a newspaper delivery boy. He looked kind of familiar. So I smiled and waved at him, but he didn't wave back. Still, that early-morning feeling was good. I wasn't even steamed like I usually am when someone doesn't wave back. People should be polite. So what if you don't know them by name or whatever?

BREAKBEAT 4
AKA KID PINK

When I got home I tried to open the front door. But it was chained from inside, so I let myself in through my bedroom window that I always kept unlocked. I tiptoed past Dad and Lori's room and figured Earl had to be at work already. I took a G.I. shower, which I always do when I'm in a rush. That's where you just wash your armpits and nothing else. Earl told me roustabouts call it a G.I. shower 'cause roustabouts and soldiers don't got enough time to take a whole shower. In the mirror I could see my right eye was getting a little black and purple where Earl tagged me. I tried to scrub the color off. Even if I pretty much knew it wouldn't work.

I locked my bike up again to the rusty old NO LOITERING AT ANY TIME signpost. I saw a crushed little bird skeleton by some weeds a couple feet from the post. I figured it had to be the same baby bird I seen on the last day of spring classes. He'd fallen from somewhere and I saw him alive and chirping. I'd scoped around for where his moms or nest might of been but wasn't able to find nothing. Mr. Johnson might of only been a part-time cookie cop. But he was a full-time a-hole. He'd come by when I was just about to pick the little bird up. It had blue on the tips of his baby wings. And a yellow throat that the bird kept wide open. But the bird's eyes couldn't barely open at all.

Johnson had told me, "His mama won't take him back you touch him."

I asked, "So, what do we do?"

Johnson raised up his right boot and grinded down hard on the little baby bird. My right hand balled into a fist, and it took all I had not to slam it hard as I could square into Johnson's nose. He sort of grinned when he saw how steamed he got me. He patted the stick holstered to his belt. "Ain't you got a class to go to, boy?" I knew I couldn't do anything. So I didn't.

For some reason, seeing the crushed little skeleton all by itself in the dirt and weeds made me sadder than the day Johnson had squashed him down. Anyway, I made it to Kaprinski's class early that day. When Alicia and her girl Teresa got there, I tried to hide the right side of my face. But Alicia saw it anyway. She looked like she almost gave a rat's poontang. "Hey, Kid. What it do?"

I played it cool. "Ah-ight."

She moved one chair closer to my right side. She leaned in. "What happened?"

"Nothing." I figured she'd drop it. But I figured wrong.

"Same door as last time?"

That got me amped. Maybe she cared. But was the way it went down really any of her business? I was all, "I guess some boppers gotta stick they nose in everything." And by "some boppers" she knew who I meant.

Her girl Teresa acted like it was for her to jump in. "Don't talk to my girl like that, *pendejo*."

I came back with a "Bite me, *pendeja*."

Then she said something in Mexican to Alicia, but she also used the word *butthole*. So I figured she was saying that's what she thought I was and wanted me to know it. Big deal.

Alicia asked Teresa, "Can you let me deal with this, T?" She touched my knee. Even though it was only my knee, I kind of jumped. Mainly 'cause I wasn't expecting it. She told me, "That stance you rolled up here with. That ain't the real you."

I shook my head. "Oh, so now you know me better than I know me." But she kept her hand on my knee and after a few seconds I started to chill. I could feel how that part of my leg got a little warmer from just her hand being there.

Mr. Kaprinski got there and started writing a lot of formulas on the blackboard.

I turned to Alicia and told her straight up, "I'll never get it."

"I think you already got it, *bebé*." The way she looked at me made me think she meant it. Not that I would ever be good at algebra and stuff, but that I could be good at something. I think that's how she meant it.

I put my hand over her hand that was on my knee. She gave me her little Alicia smile. That made it easier for me to ask. "You want to, you know, maybe do something with me? You know, maybe go somewhere or whatever sometime?"

Teresa listened in and rolled her eyes. That was probably the only thing in the whole world she was any good at. Alicia smiled at me again. "I got the who. Tell me what, where, and when."

Teresa had to chime in, "*Why* is more like it."

I didn't have anything planned out to do with Alicia.

She pretty much caught me off-guard. I just got on the gas and told her, "Umm . . . it's a surprise."

Warren shuffled in late. No Peanut. Funny as it sounds, Warren kind of had a gray look over his usual redbone color. And he mainly scoped the ground. Least he didn't look right at me during class that day. Instead of sitting in back like regular, he sat in the front of the class next to some pimple-faced geek who was always sweating in his denim jacket. The geek actually turned to Warren and grinned, like they was friends. Maybe Warren could quit Magno Clique and put together the Geek Clique.

From my side vision I spotted Alicia check me out. Real quiet-like she asked, "After class you wanna chill?"

I played dumb. "Why?"

She smiled. "It's a surprise." She was quick like that.

When class got out Warren shuffled out behind me and Alicia. I made sure to watch my back. But Warren didn't even so much as look me in the eye. I was like, "Yo, Warren. How's P doing?"

"Y'all gonna find out soon enough."

I asked him, "What's that supposed to mean?" But he just kept rolling.

I noticed that the gray look Warren had at the start of class was gone away. I don't know why but for some reason I remembered one time a few years back when he was bragging to some kids about being half Choctaw or Cherokee or Chippewa or one of them other Indian names with a Ch at the start of it.

On the way out the class I apologized to Alicia. "You were right. The stance I rolled up here with wasn't the real me."

She smiled. "Oh. So now you know you as good as I know you?"

I knew she was half gagging. Then there was the other half. How could she know so much stuff about me already when she didn't even hardly know me? Some boppers got loco radar that no guys do.

I had a question for her that was sort of hard to ask. "How 'bout you, like, invite me over to your crib or whatever?"

She smiled up at me. "Who's, like, inviting who to do what?"

I smiled back.

On the way to her house we rode beside the train tracks, over the gravel and railroad ties. I pedaled my bike and she stood on the extenders of my back wheel. Me and Alicia bounced and jiggled like Jell-O on a jack-hammer. She shouted, "Cut it out, Kid!" But the way she shouted it, you knew she dug it.

Alicia's hood was even more beat down than mine.

She held on to my shoulders and it made me feel strong. Like she was depending on my strength even more than just so she wouldn't fall off the axle extenders. And after all the practicing me and the Krew had been up to, my shoulders were getting pretty dang strong at that.

Some twanky-something black dude with a King Tut goatee was sipping from a little brown paper bag. You could tell he was a serious drink man. He watched us roll past and was like, "Yo, your sister's hot."

Most times that kind of thing might bother me. But I was in such a good mood I kept rolling and let him know, "She ain't my sister, King Tut."

King Tut shook his head. "Well, she's still hot." And I had to agree with him there.

I banked a corner and felt Alicia hang on tighter. Then I swerved the bike back and forth, time and again. Alicia held me tighter and asked, "What you doing?"

"Swangin' and bangin'." From my side vision I saw Alicia smile and shake her head. I'd never been to Alicia's house, and when I saw it I was surprised by how nice and tidy it was. I thought about how even though she lived in a worse neighborhood than me, her house was more fussed about than mine.

We slowed to a stop. Alicia hopped off the axle extenders and told me, "Hold up." She ran to her front door. I tried to look cool straddling my bike—you know how— 'cause it's all about acting caj. Like you're not hyped or stressed even when you are. She opened the front door and poked her head in. She slipped into her Mexican accent. "¿Hola, Mami?" She turned back to tell me, "It's cool."

Her living room had a big yellow sofa with one of them see-through plastic covers. And there was a lot of those church statues of the Virgin Mary and Jesus. And even some red candles.

Alicia carried in a tray from the kitchen. The tray had two glasses of tea and two ears of corn covered with mayo and some kind of red powder.

"Take one of each."

"What's the deal? The red stuff?"

"Chile pepper. Try it."

I grabbed one of the ears and chomped down. Dang, it was hot. I could feel my face go a little red. She just munched away like a typewriter. I grabbed for a glass of tea and swigged. I let her know, "This hot pepper on corn thang ain't right."

She smiled. "Huh? My little gringo can't handle it?"

She flipped through some channels with the remote till she found a music video with G-La and MC Boom.

G-La's hot, but I didn't think that was the right thing to tell Alicia. It was that song "G-La-Va-Flow." You know, the catchy little one. But I got bored watching the video. Even though G-La started to rub her booty onto Boom.

Alicia watched the TV. "She's so *bonita* . . ."

Then the video cut from G-La's booty to a mess of fruity backup dancers. Their moves were slow, all together at once, and real boring. I never got the concept of everyone dancing all together using the same moves. I mean, b-boying's about showing what makes you diff from the next guy. Like, you could be lined up with ten guys in the exact same gray flannel suit. And each one of you would stand out just 'cause of how you moved.

Alicia put her hand through my hair, but I was still scoping the TV. Her voice got sort of gripey. "What are you thinking about?"

I kept my eye on the TV. "Them guys might be getting paid, but they get no props, no respect. If them fruit loops are major, me and the Krew can be megamajor."

She leaned over and got in my grill with her little Alicia smile. "Show me *you're* not a fruit loop."

I scoped her face but was too wuss-wuss to kiss her right off. Even though I wanted to. Real bad. I told her, "You smell pretty."

"Can I ask you something personal, Kid?"

"How personal?"

"Why you do all that dance stuff with them guys? Really. I mean, no more joking."

Her saying that got me steamed. I pulled away. "Who said I'm joking? Same reason football players practice. You know, get our skills up so we can beat the comp. Someday I'm gonna do a one and a half flare suicide. And I mean do it perfect."

Talking 'bout football made me think on how, for NFL teams with serious plex, it's less about winning the Super Bowl and more about thumping the comp in your own league. Look at the Cowboys and the 'Skins. Beating the team you got serious beef with in the playoffs is the cake. Going to the Super Bowl is just the icing.

Anyway, the hardest part of the one and a half to a flare suicide is the suicide. That's where you slam onto your back all willy-nilly at the end of your set. It can be real dodgy, 'specially if you muff your timing up. I seen clips of b-boys trying to suicide onto their back but accidentally land on their head and get taken away by those emergency guys in chalk blue uniforms.

Alicia shook her head. "Yeah, but why you wanna dance in the first place?" She still didn't get it.

Instead of letting myself get more steamed, I kind of razzed her a little. "'Cause I can't rap or DJ. Why? You got something better for me to do?"

She went ahead and started kissing me, and I could taste her pink lipstick. It was kind of like those lollypops with bubble gum in the middle. But I hadn't ever really tasted anything exactly like her. She smiled and looked up at me. "My cousin Clarita's got her *quinceañera* coming up. The second Saturday of nex month. You know a gentleman I can bring as my date?"

If she wanted to gag, I could too. "Hmm . . . Warren?"

She hit me that fake way girls hit you when they want to show they're really happy. "Kid!"

I was like, "Psych. You really want me to come?"

"You need a engraved invite?"

I shook my head, leaned in, and we really mugged down. It didn't seem like a minute before there was a loud knock on the front door. Dang.

I thought it was her moms. But it was just Teresa. She acted like it was copacetic to just drop over and kick it. Even though me and Alicia didn't really want T to be there at that moment. I told you how some boppers got that special radar. Well, T wasn't one of them. Teresa was all, "Yeah, what it do? And what's Paul Dubya Junior doing up in here?"

I was like, "You wanna recognize I'm the people's champ and a chick magnet, just come out and say it. 'Sides, you more pale than me anyway. Peep that, Snow White." I held my arm, which had a lobster red sunburn, up against Teresa's.

"So, what I'm supposed to call you? Kid Pink? Actually, he looks better in lipstick, hey Alicia?"

Just then I felt the chile blazing my lips up way worse than they blazed my tongue up a few minutes before. I grabbed on my lips.

Alicia asked me, "What up? What's wrong?"

"Them chilies be hotter than Hades."

Alicia smiled and shook her head at me. "Lil' gringo can't stand the heat I bring?"

I jumped up and checked my face in the mirror. Sure thing. A bunch of pink lipstick was all over my face. I rubbed at it hard and fast as I could. And hated Teresa. Not so much for teasing me 'bout the pink lipstick but 'cause she called me Paul Wall Junior. So what if me and him were both Anglos? I guess it's a big deal to some people.

I wondered how come no one ever made fun of Trick by calling him Mike Jones Junior or whoever. I mean, they're both dark brothers, even if Trick's skinny and Jones is swoll. Then again, one time I did hear a light brother tell Trick, "You so black, you purple." I guess diff people get teased for diff things and you can't even always know the reasons why. Like how some girls get teased for wearing too much makeup at school and get called hos or whatever. And other girls get made fun of for not wearing any makeup at all and get called dykes and stuff. Dang. I guess everybody's gotta get teased about something.

BREAKBEAT 5
Ru Crawls Back

There was still a few days before Dad would get back from New Mexico. So Earl was still acting like he was the big man of the house. Shyeah, right. Like, since Dad was on the road, Earl got it in his head that he was my boss. I was always the one who had to mow the lawn and take out the trash and stuff. But when Dad was home it was diff. He made Earl do just as much as me. Maybe even more. He never said it, but I think Dad liked me more. Probably 'cause Earl could never just chill and make jokes and everything. Uptight as a vise grip. I was thinking on all that when I went to meet up with the Krew over at Mr. Bilcox's masonry yard.

Seeing Mr. Bilcox made me think how I'd only ever been over to Trick's house but three times. It wasn't that his folks wouldn't invite me in. It was more like seeing how good his family was together got me miffed thinking on how Earl and Lori were always acting a stankhole. And how my real moms was gone and stuff like that.

Trick's little sister, Lakisha, was a brainiac. Even though she was more than ten years younger than me and Trick, she was a ace at reading. Mr. Bilcox had her do it from their family Bible once in front of me. Just to show out how good she could say all the big words. Words like *atonement* and *tribulation* and *sanctification*. And other scary words that I can't even remember how they sounded let alone tell you their meanings. Lakisha'd have straight up whupped me and Trick in Miss Stringer's English class last spring. Miss Stringer was a pretty good teacher. But she was a weirdo Bible thumper and tree-hugger who told us the reason Rita put a major beatdown on B-town was 'cause God wanted to punish the B-town refineries for all the global heat they'd put up in the sky.

Anyway, one of the funny things about me and Trick was we didn't really hang in junior high. He was best friends with Big Vance back then and even all the way back in early elementary. Vance was knowed as Slim V back in elementary and on into his first year of LBJ. Then he hit his growth spurt. And I don't just mean him getting taller, but swoller— he was a skinny mug back in the day. None of that white blob belly like now. Vance was the one that introed me to Trick and Ru after he saw me b-boying around with the Fannin Street Boys. Dap had been part of the Fannin Street Boys a year before I was. Not like it's a big deal or anything, but I caught on to the harder moves even quicker than Dap. That's why the Krush Krew Trio wanted to check my skills. Trick was the main leader of the Trio, so it was for him to decide if and when I could battle my way into the Krew.

Anyway, Mr. Bilcox is Trick T's dad. He's real dark black like Trick. I wondered if back in the day anyone had ever teased Mr. B with that same line about being purple. Or worse. I rolled up to his masonry yard. It was small but megaclean and organized. Rows and rows of stacked bricks and cinderblocks and cement bags.

When I got close I saw Mr. Bilcox with a cinderblock in each hand. He stacked them on the bed of his old pickup. His face got all squirmed up and he grabbed at his lower back and rubbed it. I don't know what was wrong with his back, but it looked like it hurt pretty bad.

I got off my bike and saw Trick coming with cinderblocks. Big Vance was already there on the grass, benching a stack of four cinderblocks. And he was busting out one of his human beatbox rhythms to go along with his benching. Mr. Bilcox didn't see me yet, so I called over. "Hey, Mr. Bilcox."

He gave me that same smile like Trick has. "Hey there, Breslin." Him calling me that seemed okay. I mean, it didn't feel shiesty like when Lori said it. Mr. Bilcox peeped Vance pushing cinderblocks. "You know, you could build the same muscle helping load up this."

Vance kept benching. Didn't miss a beat. You could see his flabby white belly shake with each move. It was like a vanilla pudding with hair on it. Bucknasty. The rest of the Krew, we didn't really have chest or stomach hair. Guess Vance must of ate too much spinach and collard greens and things. I walked to the cinderblock rows. Trick gave his dad a look. "I told him he could lift here."

Mr. Bilcox put down, "I'm just pointing to facts." He turned my way and asked, "What about you, Kid? Ready to make a quick five dollars?"

I already had two blocks ready to load up. "Don't worry, Mr. Bilcox. Me and Ty gots it." Ty was Trick's birth name. Mr. Bilcox opened up his wallet and fished around. I stacked my blocks and Mr. Bilcox held out a fiver. I just nodded to Trick. "Give it to his allowance. Ty lended me five last week and I ain't paid him back yet." That was really a lie. But Trick did front me paper from time to time.

Trick looked like he was about to say something.

But Mr. Bilcox just nodded and put his paper back. "That's fine, that's fine." I guess I just figured us helping was like paying rent to use his spot for Krew practice and all.

Trick was still shooting me that look. So I went for more cinderblocks. I loaded them up and listened in on Mr. Bilcox. He used the red bandanna handkerchief he always kept parked in his front pocket to wipe sweat off his face. In a deep voice he told Trick, "Your mother 'spects you home by dinner." He said it real quiet but serious.

Trick rolled his eyes. "You already told me that already." I think Trick felt shame in his game 'cause he knew I was listening in.

Mr. Bilcox scoped Trick up and down before he walked to his van. There was a hand-painted sign on the van that said, NOTHING STACKS UP TO BILCOX MASONRY. Ru sprayed it there like two years before. Plus a copy of the same sign on the building. The other side of the building had a yellow KRUSH KREW FOR LIFE tag Ru had bombed. Ru's personal tag had used to be under the Krush Krew tag. But me and the Krew had painted over it. Like a few weeks after Ru was gone to Cali. But you could still barely make Ru's tag out under the high-gloss white we'd used.

After Mr. B was gone, Trick hissed. "Pssss. What five dollars? You know I don't get no allowance. Why you didn't take it?"

I wanted to change the subject. "I been breaking hard all this week and I know you been too."

I caught him by surprise and he was all, "How you know that?"

"'Cause you sore in the same places as me. You want me to tell you something else I know?"

Trick looked like he thought it was a trick question instead of a simple question for Trick. He was all, "Huh?"

I told him, "We so dang good, we gonna win the Throw Down." Maybe I didn't really think we could win the finals. But if we worked real real hard I figured we could take Magno Clique down. And, maybe even bigger than that, be the first crew to ever put B-town on the b-boy map. But there was another part of me that was scared. Real scared. What if Magno beat us? I couldn't even think how dissed for life the whole Krew would feel if that happened. The Clique would show out and rub our noses in it forever. We couldn't let that happen. No way, no how.

Trick wiped his face down with his sleeve and pointed at the NOTHING STACKS UP TO BILCOX MASONRY sign on the building. "Rule one, Kid. Don't stack brick less you stackin' paper." Him talking 'bout paper made me know he was fretting on if the Krew could scrape together the proper change to get to H-town and back. Five dollars more is five dollars more.

I told Trick, "Yo, the whole Krew breaks bread, we'll have the Throw Down scrilla furilla." If all three of us stacked our change and paper together we'd for sure have enough.

Trick was all, "Whatever. I dropped twanky just on vinyl last week." Twanky and twenty are the same number, but you'd never catch Miss Stringer saying "twanky."

Trick kept going. "Got me Michael 5K Watts screwin' and choppin' the latest Mike Jones—ya feel me, son?" He motioned over the two cinderblock spaces like a DJ mixing. That reminded me how Warren had wanted to be a DJ too. Before he joined up with Magno. Trick was like, "And y'all know we been slacking on our grind. We gotta practice daily for the Throw Down."

Big Vance came over all sweaty and swoll and heavy breathing. Since Vance was professional chilling, me and Trick took a little breather too.

Vance did some jellyrolls just to gag around. But me

and T were too tired to chuckle. Vance put down, "We'll be so dang good, maybe even get scouted or sponsored like Magno Clique was smacking on about."

I threw out, "True that. We really grind then we can shine, even win the motha."

Trick shook his head. "Man, we don't gotta win, so long as we mash and represent." He waited a long second then asked, "Y'all really think we ready this year?"

I came back with, "If X equals one hundred percent, then I'm X times a factor of two for sure."

Trick asked, "How much is that?"

"That's two hundred percent for sure."

Trick was impressed. "Dang, that's a lot."

I never thought Mr. Kaprinski's algebra would help the Krew get psyched for the Throw Down. Almost made me want to bone up on my homework. But there was more important stuff to do that night. For one thing there was practice. For another thing there was a *caliente* date with Alicia. She taught me the word *caliente* and it means "hot" in Mexican. She taught me some other words too. But a lot of them I might get in trouble for if I told you about. 'Specially if it ever got back to her moms.

Me and Trick loaded up the last cinderblocks. It was so many they near 'bout filled the truck bed past its brim.

Trick fell back onto the grass next to Vance. I was tired too. But like I said, there was important stuff to do. I scoped a double-wide section of plywood lying on the ground. I asked Trick and Vance, "Can y'all drop any new moves?" They acted asleep but I told them, "Peep this." I went headfirst for the plywood. I landed good and busted into a ol'-skool windmill. I went clockwise and spun around and around. From shoulder to shoulder and back again, feet up in the air. Things rotated around so fast, I got that good feeling in my guts. Like everything was right and nothing was wrong. Spinning and spinning like the original Spindletop way back in the day.

I heard Vance. He sounded real far away. "That junk ain't boss." Like he was Slim Thug or somebody.

But Trick had my back. "He done changed it up. Like to see you jump a windmill your whack self."

A windmill's a ol'-skool move. But it took me like six months to really get my basic rotation pretty tight. Then you change up your windmill by doing diff things. Like putting your hands way up on your hips. They call that eggbeaters. Or you can grab your pickle during your windmills. Those are called nutcrackers and are a good way to dis the comp. Come to think of it, grabbing your nutsack pretty much anytime is a good way to dis whoever.

I was running out of steam and I heard Trick break out with a cheer. "Go B, go B, go B, go B . . ." Even Vance joined in. After I knew I couldn't keep the windmill going I ended with a spread-eagle freeze. With a freeze you just stop moving and stay rock still. Even though I was in freeze mode the sky spun around and around.

I smiled up at the clouds. "Wait till I bust that on Magno."

Big Vance was all, "Magno Clique can smoke my johnson *and* lick my nutsack." Everybody chuckled.

Next, Trick was on deck. I got up and high-fived him. He kicked out some uprock footwork, which wasn't regular for him. Footwork's more about getting into the groove and setting yourself up to do groundwork. Or else so you can catch your breath during competition. Big Vance busted out some human beatbox, which sounded as good as the ol'-skool Fat Boys tapes we used to break to.

Trick got into a headstand and did a headspin that kept going and going. I gave him a chant over Vance's human beatbox. "Go T, go T, go T, go T, go T . . ."

Trick's headspin must've lasted at least fifteen seconds. Okay, ten. He dropped to his back and gave that Trick smile. "H-Town Throw Down, gonna get K-rushed."

Trick rolled off the board. Vance high-fived him and threw down some big solo uprock of his own. Uprock's where you basically put down footwork with your feet, plus kung fu–type moves with your arms. But you can't touch whoever you're battling. For practice you can do it solo like a shadowboxer. That's what Vance was up to.

Me and Trick were all, "Go V, go V, go V, go V, go V . . ." Vance wormed across the plywood diagonal. Then Big V broke into a backspin that ended with a goofy stylin' pose. Me and Trick just busted up laughing. One thing 'bout b-boying's that you don't gotta have all the best moves. If you can have a good time and make people laugh, it's almost as good. That's why Vance was still part of the Krew. Not 'cause of his skills. No offense, Big V.

Trick looked away from the plywood and his face got serious. I clocked where he was looking and saw Izzle, Dap, Peanut, and Warren tip by all slow-like in Dap's candy red El C. That was the first I seen Peanut since the fight in back of the school. I was glad he was doing okay. But I felt my stomach tighten up. You know, prep for something to go down. Vance jumped right up. All set to throw down.

The El C had the subwoofers thumping screwed and chopped. Dap was swangin', swerving the slab back and forth across the road. Then he started bangin', making the ride go side to side real jerky and quick. Warren and

Izzle were sittin' sideways, hanging out the windows with Styrofoam cups.

Trick shook his head. "Dap fittin' to wreck that slow loud and banging."

Vance motioned to the seventeen-inch rims. "Lots of bass, but them block-beaters sittin' on minors."

Dap slammed to a stop and turned the bass down a touch. The Magno Clique stepped out.

Peanut's face was puffy. He had on a bunch of cheap bandages. Like his moms or auntie or someone else that wasn't a real nurse had stuck them on.

Whenever he talked, Izzle made sure to flaunt the princess cuts and invisible sets in his top grill. "Iz da K R ush K R ta tha izzew ready ta fizzight?"

Vance stepped up and grabbed at his nutsack. "Kick rocks or come get some! Y'all faggots want more of this? Huh?"

Izzle grinned even wider and put his hands up. "Yo, we J to tha izzust clockin' for a friendly neighborhood battle. If y'all's dizz-own." Dang. From the whack way he talked you'dve thunk Izzle came up in Long Beach, not Port Arthur.

I looked from Trick to the Magno Clique. "Battle? Right here, right now?"

Izzle was like, "Whenever, crackizzle."

I whispered to Trick, "That means cracker in izzle-talk, don't it?"

Trick rolled his shoulders up like he didn't know. Even if he probably did. I nodded. "Hell shyeah, we ready to stunt."

Warren asked, "When, son?"

I told him, "Nex week. Same time, same place."

Magno Clique talked so we couldn't hear them. They started to get back in the El C. Izzle pointed at me.

"Coolio, cave bro." Cave bro being another way to say wigger.

Trick had my back by shouting out, "Y'all can't shake the block sittin' on minors." That was a full on dis. Even if it's true any rims under eighteen inches are minors. Dap gave Trick a ugly mug, which was funny to see coming from a Oriental dude like Dap. Then he cranked the bass up and peeled out.

Vance clocked the Clique till they swanged around the corner and out of sight. "At least they got a slab. Yo, peep that."

Vance motioned to a dude on a yellow Viper Diamond-back trick bike rounding the corner. I scoped Trick. I could tell he was thinking the same thing as me. That it was Ruina. I told Trick, "I thought he was still in the three twenty-three."

Ruina pulled his hood back and rolled over. "Yo, Kid. Yo, Trick."

I was like, "Say, mane. Thought you was still in Cali."

Ruina used to be pretty light-skinned. He was a lot more tan than last time we seen him. And he had a little gold earring with a feather in his left ear. Even though Ru spoke good Mexican, only his moms's side was from there. His moms was Mexican and his dad was full Navajo from some Indian rez out in Arizona. But his dad had a Navajo wife. He never married his moms and only called Ru but once every four years. On Ru's leap year b-day.

Before he left for Cali, Ru told me how his moms moved them from city to city and learned him Mexican, and even some Navajo. As a kid in Albuquerque, Ru only ever spoke Mexican since he'd got beat down time and again by kid *esés* for being Indian. He told me how he'd even went so far as to join up with a gang of junior *esés*. He took the nickname Ruina and fronted like he was 100 percent Mexican. By the time him and his moms moved to Beaumont he had the *esé* act down cold. Everyone but the Krew got fooled.

Anyway, Ru scoped me and Trick and V and asked,

"What it do?" He put out his right elbow but the three of us fronted like we didn't even notice. "Yo, Kid. Yo, Trick." Ruina scoped over at the masonry building where his graff name had got painted over and was like, "What happened to my tag?"

Trick rolled his shoulders up. "My daddy wasn't having it no more."

Ru's elbow was still out. "Oh really. He was here when I bombed it. Y'all gonna leave me hanging?"

And we did leave him hanging. Trick scoped the clock in his dad's office and put down, "Yeah. Sort of like how you left the Krew dangling just before last year's H-Town Throw Down." Trick got on his bike. "I'll catch y'all on the flip side." He rolled off.

Ruina looked more sad than pissed. I tried some small chatter with him. "What happened to the bike sponsorship?" You could see he didn't want to answer that one.

He was all, "You *chicas* wanna talk sponsorship, then tell me y'all's ready for the Throw Down. I picked up a gang of krump moves out West . . ." Still straddling his bike, Ruina shook out a few krump-style chest pops.

Vance ignored Ruina and was like, "Don't know 'bout that, but I'm ready ta whup Kid's booty on 'Tendo."

I looked at the ground. "Yo, Ru. I gots ta blaze."

"You too, Kid?"

"You can't just roll back into the Krew right before H-town, like how you rolled out last summer. You know how it is."

"Nah. Not really. How is it?"

"It is what it is."

Wheeling off with Vance, I thought on how Ru's moms hadn't moved them to Beaumont till after Ru was already done with elementary. And nobody in the Krew knew the particulars about what it was like for Ru growing up here and there all over the map. With no other Indians around and no real dad. I think that's how Ru liked to keep it. When he was part of the Krew, if you asked him how things were for him back in the early days, as a rule he'd just change the subject to this or that or another thing. Me and V chunked the deuce. I could still feel Ru hating on me when I banked around the corner to the North.

The up-est thing I remember 'bout that day was when I crossed the train tracks. The Sunset Limited was passing East, and a real pretty girl with bright red hair and a yellow flower in it looked out the window and smiled at me. It was all sort of fast, so maybe it wasn't me she was smiling at. But I'd bet a dollar to a dime on it. Keep it on the low, 'cause Alicia might go a little loco on me, hearing 'bout stuff like that. I still can't tell you why bops go loco on you for no good reason. But I'm working on it. If you already got it figured out, gimme a holler and lemme know.

BREAKBEAT 6
MEXICAN FOR ALICE

When I got home the door was chained from the inside again. Earl. I heard myself talk out loud. "Dong-smoking dicksmith Dookie of Earl." Someone had locked my bedroom window too. Probably Lori. So I had to sneak in through the little laundry room window. When I went down the hall I heard Lori moaning and stuff. I know it's kinda off, but I stopped at Lori's door and listened in for a piece. I could picture Earl all on top of Lori. And both of them all sweaty. I heard enough of that and went to Earl's room. The door creaked. It made me freeze. Just for a second. But Lori was still ooing and aaing, so I knew it was safe.

The little four-point buck Earl shot when he was twelve stared at me from its place over his old Vince Young poster. He thought it was a major deal back then and would even floss today if you asked him 'bout it. Me, I never could get why you'd want to cap a nice quiet animal like a deer. Let alone stuff its head and hang it on the wall. Anyway, his old motocross trophy was on the left edge of the dresser. I was there to borrow some dress clothes 'cause mine were all hand-me-downs of his anyway. But everything in my closet was too small.

Most his dress stuff was Wal-Mart type. Pants and short-sleeve shirts. And he had a whole wooden box full of them shiny dress shoes. I took a pair of them light brown pants. Keekees, I think they call it. And a white long-sleeve. I took my gear off in front of Earl's dresser mirror. I tried his stuff on. It was funny to see me in dress clothes. 'Specially 'cause they were way baggy on me. I already told you, Earl's got forty pounds on me. Mostly muscle.

I grabbed for a bottle of Jordan cologne on the dresser. I sprayed three squirts on my neck. I could hear Lori ooing again. Even through the wall. I checked my reflection while I put the cologne back on the dresser. *Bang!* I looked down and saw Earl's motocross trophy busted in half on the floor. Lori's moaning stopped on a dime. It was hard to hear exactly what Earl said through the wall. Something like, "What the hell?"

I made a run for the closet. Then I remembered I forgot my gear on the floor. I ran back, grabbed it up, and hid in the closet. I had the closet door shut most the way just when Earl kicked open the door to his room. He sweated all over and was naked 'cept for some sheet with little green flowers on it. I could see he had something in his right hand. His aluminum baseball bat. Oh, mane. I guess he thought a robber was in the house, 'cause he was all, "Who's there? I got a gun, you sum-buck."

Then, real careful, he patrolled around the room till he saw his busted-up motocross trophy. "Damn it! Breslin?"

Why'd he have to blame me right off? Even if it was me who broke it doesn't mean he had to blame me right off like that. I seen him drop on his hands and knees and look under his bed. You could see the greasy old deflatable doll he kept there. Couldn't believe he still had it. I mean, he'd been sweating Lori for more than a year. Plus, he had a baker's dozen naked-lady tapes under the bed too. I wondered how much I could sell them for. Earl scoped the closet and I thought he seen me but wasn't sure. I backed up farther into it, behind the shirts.

Nothing but a bunch of Earl's shirts in my grill, so I couldn't really see. I heard the closet door open. I held my breath. After a few seconds the closet door closed. Must've fooled the Dookie of Earl. To be sure, I chilled for what seemed a long hour. Even if it was probably only two minutes. Once I got out the closet I heard Lori again so I knew Earl was in there with her, doing his thing. Funny thing was I never heard Earl leave his room. He was a natural sneak.

I heard bits of Lori saying stuff like "Oh yeah, do that thing. Mmm, right there. Okay, baby, right there. Yes!" And some other things that it's hard to remember exactly. Plus, I probably shouldn't talk about them kind of things anyway.

Part of me was real steamed at Earl for doing that stuff. Dad would kill him if he knew. A way smaller part of me was steamed at Earl 'cause I kind of wished she wanted me to do that to her instead of him. I only felt that for like two seconds. Then I just felt bad about the whole thing and wished we could be like them families you see in them old black-and-white TV shows. Where everyone just acts regular and stuff.

I took a pair of Earl's shiny dress shoes and got out of there quiet and quick. On my way to Alicia's I had to work hard to get the pictures of Lori and Earl out of my head, which was funny. 'Cause I only heard them doing it through the wall and never even seen them.

Halfway to Alicia's I took a corner real tight and almost wrecked. But it wasn't my fault. It was 'cause Earl's shoes was way too big on me and it was hard to pedal. I saw King Tut in his usual place with his usual brown paper bag. And of course he had to say the usual thing. "Yo, where's your sexy sister?"

I shook my head and told him, "She ain't my sister," which was dumb 'cause I knew what he'd say next anyway.

Yup. Sure enough. "She still sexy . . ."

Him saying that, even though I knew he'd say it, got me real pissed. Don't ask me the reason. I slammed the brakes on my bike and skidded out to a stop. "Say it again."

He played it like, "Say what?"

I was like, "The same trash you always talk."

He got a little scared. "I don't know what you talkin' 'bout." I knew he did, but since he kind of backed down I decided to keep wheeling to Alicia's. Just after I turned the first corner I heard him yell out after me, "Peckerwood!"

When I rolled up to Alicia's I could hear some Mexican-type music coming from across the street. It was real pretty. The kind of music that made you want to dance but not break. I already told how I got that Fred Astaire poster on the wall. Me and all the Krew like some of his style. Even if it's old and he sometimes dances like a punk. Nobody wants to listen to the story part of a dance movie. So we always just fast-forward to the good stuff.

That's what someone told me people also do with them naked-lady type movies. But I wouldn't know 'bout that.

Anyway, the music from across the way made me think of Fred Astaire. Going up the steps to Alicia's front door, I kind of tried some of his moves. But I stopped in the middle of the stairway 'cause I saw Alicia's moms. Yeah. Mrs. Guerrero was peeking through a window. Dang. Busted. I like it when people see me break. But dancing kind of fruity like that, well, it wasn't the same.

She opened the door and I was like, "I was just . . . Hi, Mrs. Guerrero."

Alicia came up behind her moms. She was more fine than I ever seen her up to then. She had on a hella fine blue dress. She was all, "You look nice!" That was the first time she seen me in dress clothes. And maybe it was also 'cause I had my hair watered back. She kind of showed me her moms and said, "My moms. *Señora* Guerrero de Hernandez."

"Mrs. Guerrero de Hern . . . Herna . . ." I tried to say it like Alicia did but couldn't.

Her moms introed herself. "I'm Xenia. You're the math student?" She asked the question like I did something wrong. Or there was something she didn't get.

And me, I was a little throwed by the math student

question. Like, who did Alicia tell her I was? I put my hand out. "Kid B. Or you can call me Breslin." She put her hand in mine but didn't really shake.

Alicia kind of turned around and showed me her dress and everything. She asked me how she looked. I'd be lying if I didn't say how good she looked. Truly. I told her, "Better than the best, *bebé*." Her moms kind of stepped back when she saw how I was scoping on her daughter. I didn't mean to stare her up and down like that. But I guess I did.

The next thing to go down really put some shame in my game. 'Cause I was wearing Earl's pants, and they were real baggy and all, you could see real easy when my pickle got woken up. It kind of made a little teepee or whatever. I mean, not to floss, but it was kind of a swoll teepee and swollin' up more and more right then and there. I didn't mean it to happen. It just pretty much happened all on its own. Without me even trying to think about it or something.

I turned to try and hide it. But her moms must've scoped it. "Before I invite you into my home, I want you to promise me one thing, Breslin."

"Yes'm?"

She peeped me right in the eye like a marine sergeant

or whatever. "Promise me that you won't sleep with my baby while she's living under my roof."

Alicia was like, *"Mami!"*

I scoped the ground 'cause it was too hard to look at Alicia's moms. I forced myself to look up. "Yes'm. I mean, no, ma'am. I wouldn't do that." Man, it felt like twanky questions even if there were no questions.

"Promise me."

I felt a big throat frog sitting on my Adam's apple. Leesha jumped in again, "Mom! Leave him be. I told you. We're just study buddies." That seemed kind of funny. I knew Leesha didn't think of me as just a friend. And for dang sure didn't think of me as a bookworm. I could tell her moms wasn't buying it neither.

I got the throat frog to jump off my Adam's apple and told her moms, "I promise I won't have, umm, sleep with, your daughter in this house." All that stressing put my pocket rocket back to sleep right quick. It finally seemed like everything was copacetic.

But her moms kept on. "While she's living under my roof."

Sheesh. "While she's living under your roof, ma'am."

Mrs. Guerrero smiled and opened the door. "Welcome."

I felt a little red in the face. When I stepped inside I got to thinking how even though Alicia's dad was gone, her house was almost like one of them black-and-white TV shows. Where everyone just acts regular and stuff.

Mrs. Guerrero had real nice food and I ate it all. Even asked for seconds on everything. Not like with the kind of slop Lori always made. First thing we had was soup with tortillas instead of noodles. There was also stuff in the soup like onions and cheese and chili and a bunch of things I couldn't even tell you 'bout 'cept that they tasted 100.

I had a Coke from Mexico that tasted better than the Coke we Anglos get. Sort of like how the Dr Pepper from Dublin, Texas, tastes better than other Dr P's 'cause they use real sugar instead of that sweet corn sauce stuff. And Leesha let me sip her *horchata*. It's a tasty rice drink, but was way too sweet for me.

After dinner was finished Mrs. G brought out hot chocolate that used 100 percent milk and no water. After all the good eating I could tell Mrs. Guerrero thought I should be rolling out. I wanted to chill with Alicia all night. I kept thinking how nice it would be to give her a kiss good night. Or even mug down. Leesha walked me to the door and shut it. So her moms couldn't see. I put my arms around Leesha and she got ready for a kiss. Then I scoped her moms peeking out the window. Busted again.

"Don't look now, but your moms be clockin' us from the window."

"Okay, study buddy. See you in class."

Even with her moms peeping us, Leesha got on her tippy-toes and kissed me. Just on the cheek. But it still made me feel way better than those times I kissed Cajun style with Cassie Morrison way back in freshman year. Maybe it was 'cause Cassie always had breath that tasted like five-day-old hamburger meat. Cassie was the first girl I ever really mugged down with, so I thought all girls might taste that way. At least up until I played truth or dare with Madison Gumtree in second year.

I was surprised not to see King Tut like usual when I rolled past his spot. But after I wheeled the corner to my block, I got a real surprise. There it was. Dad's big rig. It could carry two swimming pools full of gasoline at once. And there he was. Climbing out of the rig. The lower part of his shoulder tattoo popped out from under his left short sleeve. It was a Marine tattoo and had some old language that said SEMPER FI. He told me what it meant once but I forgot. I think it was something 'bout staying together with your team or whatever.

Dad's got one of those faces like you see cowboys have in the ads. No fat on it and kind of dried up from being outside in the sun maybe too much. I was just real happy he was back home a few days early. I rotated my pedals fast as I could with Earl's big shoes on. "Dad, why're you—I thought . . ."

Dad turned with a full on grin. "Hey, pistol." His smile's one of those kinds that make you smile too. Even when you don't want to. Kind of like the way Trick and Mr. Bilcox smile. I dropped my bike and gave him a bear hug.

"All right, all right . . ." He pushed me away and scoped Earl's clothes up and down. "You just come from church?"

"I thought . . . Earl said you wasn't getting back till . . ."

"Well? If it ain't church, who is she?" Dad was smart like that.

"She's a nice girl, Dad. Alicia."

His forehead sort of crinkled. "Ain't that Mexican for Alice?"

All I could think to say was "I guess." Which sort of made me feel bad. Like I didn't have Leesha's back or something.

Dad nodded and motioned to the left side of the rig. "One of 'em's low. Grab the nigger stick."

I didn't like how Dad called it that, and when I jumped into the cab I punched the dashboard. Hard. It hurt like all get out, but I only skinned three knuckles. I scoped around for the tire stick. It's basically a mini—baseball bat. Like a police guy's nightstick or whatever. The cab was full of empty cans of Lone Star. Two empty bottles of J.T.S. Brown. Here and there some pickle wrappers. Didn't make any sense, 'cause Lori never trucked with Dad.

I thought about Alicia in that little blue dress before dinner. One of the pickle wrappers even had a plastic mouth on it that said FRENCH TICKLER. I wondered if it was some Cajun just over the state line who invented it. Maybe even that same cat who named Beaumont. I found the tire stick and tested the tires. Sure enough, four pair down, the outer one was soft. "Found it."

"Earl can take it down to Randy's tomorrow. I been driving three days straight. I'm starving."

Dad sparked up a Winston and started for the house. Then it hit me. Earl was probably still in Dad and Lori's room. I ran in front of him and was like, "Dad, hold up. I got your b-day present out in the living room. You ain't 'upposed to see it yet." Of course that was a lie. But I had to tell it.

He shook his head and stopped in the middle of the front yard. "That's a month off. All right, Kid." Just before I got to the door he was all, "And put some coffee on. Chicory."

I couldn't open the door. Earl still had it chained from inside. I stuck my mouth through the crack in the door. I tried to whisper loud enough so Earl could hear me. "Earl. *Earl*. Get up. *Get up*." Dang, I didn't think he could hear me. Dad would kill him. And maybe Lori too. Then I heard some lazy footsteps coming to the front door. The door shut for a second. I heard the chain slide off its track. Earl yanked open the door. He still had that sheet with green flowers around his waist. I could hear cheese-ass soul music in the background. Earl's eyes were puffy. Like I must've woke him up.

It didn't take him but a second to say, "What the hell? That's my clothes, you little mooch-weasel."

I kept my voice quiet. "I ain't a mooch-weasel. And you better clean up whatever you doing. *Dad's* home."

"What the?" Earl scoped over my shoulder at the tanker and knew I wasn't messing with him. He looked real scared. He hustled to warn Lori. I could hear him saying, "God dang! God dang!"

Dad didn't come in till I told him I had the present hid. If he knew the real story maybe he'd want to kill me too. I got out the chicory coffee. It's the only kind Dad likes 'cause his side comes from Louisiana. Even from the kitchen I could hear Dad knocking on the bathroom door in his bedroom. Lori must have locked herself in there to clean up her whatever. I heard her front all nice to Dad. "What is it, sweetie?"

"Open up in there. I'm gonna pee my pants." Lori didn't say nothing back and a few seconds later Dad was all, "Get out here and take these boots off, woman."

I could barely hear her: "Yeah. Whatever you want, shit-ass." Even though she didn't mean it. 'Cept the shit-ass part. That was Lori's favorite word when Dad was home. Real original.

Dad ate some of Lori's bad mac and cheese. She sat at the table but didn't say anything. I poured a coffee for me. I was glad I was still full up from Mrs. Guerrero's stuff. I liked watching Dad eat. It was a few weeks from the last time we seen him. But Lori looked at him like she was steamed he was back at his house. The house he paid most all the rent on. Like more than double what Earl paid.

Dad wolfed down the mac and cheese and grabbed a refill of the coffee I made. When he sipped it he squinted real serious. Like he was judging a small-batch bourbon competition. "You did it right, Kid. Not too much water."

Lori squirmed like it was meant as a dis on her. Which it kind of was. I tried not to smile on the outside. But I think she caught the shit-eating grin I felt growing on my face. She didn't have a comeback for him like she sometimes does. She just kept quiet. Real quiet.

Dad asked me, "How's that class you're in?"

I told him, "It's good, it's going good. I should be graduated this summer." That was a flat-out lie. Even if I did pass Mr. Kaprinski's class. Well, I mean, I *should* be graduated, but in reality I *wouldn't* be. It was my fourth year in high school. But I still only had enough credits that the career counselor, Mr. Molina, said I was basically just a second-semester freshman. Dad and Lori never checked my grades like my real moms used to. So it was easy to keep everything on the low.

Dad got all serious. "Good. It's important. That credential will last you a lifetime. Hell, soon as you got that diploma, they'll take you at the refinery. Like your brother."

That took the shit-eater off my face. "Yeah" was all I could get out my mouth.

Earl teased me, "First he's gotta grow some muscle."

The teasing didn't bother me near so much as thinking on what if I *did* have to work at the refinery with Earl. That would suck donkey sack. Truly. So what if Vance's dad was a foreman and might have my back? With no diploma I'd get paid even less than they started Earl at. And have a worse work detail than him. But the diploma thing itself didn't stress me. I figured even being king honcho college boy of the refinery would suck near as bad. No matter what Mr. K said about b-boying just being a hobby, that's not what it was to me. There had to be some way to get down, get props, and get paid. I was already on the grind. And set to grind harder. If them cheese balls on TV could do it, I could do it too. And do it better.

Dad scoped around at the mess in the dining room and on into the kitchen. He peeped over at Lori and shook his head. "I bring my money home to a pigsty. There's a God-awful stink all over the place. Mind me asking why?" Lori didn't even answer him so he kept on. "You seen a doctor about that laryngitis?"

That got Lori's goat, 'cause she was like, "Chet, you're a tiresome prickweed. Tiresome. You got it?"

"Yeah, I got it. You're tired of sitting on your ass bone all day. Or is it codeine again?"

Earl stepped in, "Daddy . . ."

"What?" Dad scoped Earl laser hard. That pretty much shut him up.

Earl looked down at his plate, way scared. "Umm. Nothing, sir."

The only time Earl ever called Dad "sir" was when he was worried he was gonna catch a beating. I never called Dad that. Maybe 'cause Dad never put a serious beatdown on me like he sometimes did Earl.

Lori stood and looked down at Dad. Her face got cold and still. "Everybody here likes you more when you're passed out."

You could see Dad's jaw working, which meant he was real mad. About to blow. Lori walked off real calm to the bedroom. All three of us sat there quiet. Not knowing what to say. I was about to try and say something. Nothing came out.

Dad pushed his plate away from hisself. At Earl. Dad cleared his throat and fronted like he wasn't mad 'cause of how Earl sort of started to call him on how he talked to Lori. Dad's voice got real low and quiet. "Outside right third—no, fourth tire's low. And we got a idle problem."

Earl jumped right in on the new subject. "Okay. But you know Randy's offshore till, I don't know . . . Saturday?" Randy was one of Dad's oldest buddies and he always looked after the rig when it needed fixing. I think

Randy's also my godfather. But I'm not 100 on that. What I can tell you for sure is I never got a single present or card or anything from Randy. Or whoever it is that might be my godfather.

I must've been a little jittery, 'cause I spilled a big splash of coffee across Earl's dress shirt when I sipped. "Goddamn, Kid. That's my only no-wrinkle long-sleeve."

"Sorry, Earl." But I was laughing when I said it. And I mean laughing loud. And I laughed for a good long minute, like someone had told the funniest gag of the year or something.

Dad peeped over at me and flashed that full on grin of his. I guess he thought the whole thing was funny too. Then I got a idea of how I might have some giggles by messing with Earl a little. I'd scare him but not really bust him. "Hey, Earl. Why don't you tell Dad about your new lady friend?"

Dad asked, "Oh yeah? Who's the new chippy?"

Earl told him, "You wouldn't know her."

Dad gave Earl another one of his laser stares. "Maybe I would."

Earl kicked my leg pretty solid. And I told him, "Do it again. Go ahead."

Earl tried to get me back in front of Dad. "First get up

on the table and show us your latest jigaboo move." Dad looked from Earl to me.

Dad was set to ask me something. But I jumped in first and told Earl, "I don't know what you're talking 'bout, Romeo."

Dad shook his head. "All right, all right. Each of you clowns simmer down now."

BREAKBEAT 7
THE SECRET SPOT

Next day, I ran through the lime grove where my Paw Paw used to take me before he died. He told about how he worked picking limes back when the oil business was slow and they still grew limes and stuff like that in Beaumont. I wasn't but eight when he spent a whole day showing me how to drive his Farmall H cotton tractor. Me and him prepped the little field in back of his house. Three days after he showed me, they found him in his driveway. In the front seat of his Ford. Something had attacked his heart. And his dead body flopped forward and made the horn honk and honk until somebody heard it and found him.

Anyway, there's a lot of undergrowth in the lime grove. No one tends to the orchard anymore. But the limes still grow. I found the biggest tree in sight and grabbed the strongest branch. I think I managed fifteen or sixteen pull-ups. I told Alicia 'bout the orchard, but I didn't know if she'd like it same as I did. Even in the middle of day it was always a little spooky 'cause no one else ever went there.

Back when I was twelve I remember seeing a dead mule under one of the lime trees. It didn't make any sense 'cause there were no farms next to the orchard. But I saw what I saw. There was a old dirt road through the middle of the orchard with a bunch of special old trees, way bigger than the limes. They were 'bout the only tall trees in B-town whose tops hadn't got chewed off by Rita. And they smelled really pretty 'cause a lot of flowers grew on them. It was that kind of real quiet place where you could just go and not stress about anything. There's none too many places like that.

It took me like twanky minutes to bike to Larson's Pawn. Mostly 'cause my backpack slid off a bunch of times. I seen the shop a few times before. It was just on the edge of Magnolia, so I had to watch my six. When I went inside there was a bunch of bells on the door that jingled. Behind the counter was a old man with those half-lens-type glasses. He chewed on a toothpick. Mr. Larson, I figured.

He peeped over his half-lens glasses rims. On the counter was a case with a bunch of cheap pistols. The most rickety one had a busted-up handle that was all wound up with red electrical tape.

The old geezer asked me, "Watch? Radio? What you need?"

"Y'all carry any hip-hop gear? I got some tapes to flip."

"Okay, hip-hopper. What you got? Gray tapes, or your daddy's old eight tracks?"

"Nah. Check it."

I dug into my backpack. I stacked all thirteen of Earl's naked-lady tapes on the counter.

The old man shook his head. "Fitty cent apiece."

"That's all?"

"Ain't you got the memo? We living in the digital age, son."

The old man put a bottle of Windex on the counter.

"Clean them greasy things off. Then I'll pay you."

I did like he told me to. The bunch of them only came to six dollars fifty, but the old man gave me seven.

On Monday Wes was kicking it the boys' room like always. Flossin' his gold tooth with the princess cut to hisself in the mirror. He jiggled a bottle of muddy lemon-lime and asked, "Where's my paper?"

I yanked out five dollars without even thinking. Then I pocketed the five right back and shook my head. "You ain't gonna like what I'm doing. I ain't sippin' no more. I'm in grind mode. Feel me?"

Wes got throwed. "Nah. Not really."

"Me and the Krew gonna hit H-Town Throw Down nex month and rep B-town."

Wes grinned. "Well, then. Do it to it, bigtimer. Make B-town shine."

Wes put his fist out. I knocked mine against his and told him, "Already."

Starting that Monday, Peanut was back in Mr. Kaprinski's class. His face was still puffy and he still wore them cheap bandages that looked like his moms or auntie slapped them on. Him and Warren came over to me after class. Alicia was up in front talking to Mr. Kaprinski. Peanut peeped at me through his bandages. I scoped him right back.

Peanut held out his right hand like he wanted to make peace. "Yo, 'preciate it, Kid."

"Huh?"

"You know. Warren told me 'bout what went down after things went black. I know you had my back. Feel me?"

"No doubt."

Peanut chunked me the deuce. Warren was all, "Heard y'all gonna foshizzle hit the H-Town Throw Down nex month."

"I don't know." I had to play it cool 'cause I didn't know what they were about.

Alicia and Teresa walked up and Peanut and Warren stepped back. Warren pointed at me, but friendly. "Ah-ight, Kid. We out."

I was like, "Shyeah."

I walked Alicia to the door and I told her, "Let's roll to my special spot. But only if you keep it on the low."

She got a devilish grin and patted me a little down around my nads. "Special spot? Where? Here?"

Teresa rolled her eyes. "I *so* didn't see that."

I spotted Kaprinski looking over and told Alicia to cut it out. Teresa got hissy-pissy with Alicia. "I thought we was going to Crockett Street."

Alicia looked confused. "I thought that was tomorrow."

Teresa pulled out her moms's car keys. "Got the *mami*'s Caprice all week. So where's this stupid special place we rolling to?"

I got steamed. Her saying it that way and acting like she could just invite herself along with me and Alicia. I was like, "Can't you just take a hint, dumb-dumb? Ride or no ride, you a third wheel." Which was true, 'cause who cared if she had her moms's station wagon?

Teresa peeped Alicia, then me. "Who said I even want to go to your stupid place anyway?" She talked some Mexican to Alicia, but the only words I could catch was *redneck* and *trastero*. Alicia had told me that last one means "anus" in Mexican. Like I even gave a plug buffalo nickel what Teresa thought. Teresa must of knowed that Leesha thought she was a third wheel too. She clomped off down the hall all in a huff.

I could tell that Alicia felt bad about it, so I felt a little bad too. Leesha was all, "Kid. I know you don't wanna kiss her, but you don't gotta dis her." I gave Leesha my best *What'd I do?* look. You know the one.

Me and Alicia had already done more than hold hands before. But being out in the lime grove holding her hand was something diff. Neither of us said anything for a long minute. We just walked and walked. That's part of what I liked about her. You could just be quiet with her but it wasn't funny or off or anything.

She looked around. "It's so quiet."

I told her, "Yeah. My Paw Paw worked here picking limes, back when he was alive." I pointed out the dirt road. "And over there's a old dirt road with some special trees. That's how come it's my special place."

It was funny hearing myself say that. Like maybe I was telling her too much. Maybe she would laugh at me. But she didn't laugh. She let me take her over a small hill to the road. It was old and made of dirt. But the nice thing was those special trees that smelled real good. The sun was so strong, it came through the tree leaves real bright and made everything glow green. Then Leesha had to ruin things by harping on about Teresa.

I was like, "She's always up in our grill and stuff."

"We've been best friends since forever."

"How'd she get to be so clueless?"

"Don't call her that. Diego don't ever call from Port Arthur. Got her head all messed up. She been forgotten."

"Sounds like a personal problem to me."

"Hey, Kid. Around me, you don't have to act all hard."

"I don't know what you're talking 'bout."

"Oh, I think you do."She tried to change the subject. "It smells like real expensive perfume."

I went along. "Yeah, it's them flowers on the trees. Hold up." I shimmied up the tree like a monkey. That's something I always been pro at. I mean shimmying up trees, not acting a monkey. I broke off the twig with the freshest flower I could grab. I got down and gave it to her. She smiled more sweet than even that *horchata* drink she let me try at dinner that time.

She smelled at the flower. Then scoped my face like she wanted me to kiss her. I did kiss her. And right on the lips too. Real slow-like and soft, she backed up from kissing me. Her eyes looked up and down and over my face. "We're not under my mom's roof right now."

I was like, "Yeah, but you still *live* under her roof."

"Whatever. How much you like me? I mean, really like me."

"Do you gotta ask?"

"Then why you gotta be all technical?"

"I gave your moms my word. Besides the Krew, that's all I got."

She pushed me that soft way girls do. "Your crew and your word's all you got? What about me?"

"No. What do you mean?"

I tried to come up with something that sounded good. But I couldn't. Leesha looked up at me. "What are you thinking?"

"Want me to tell you 'bout my best move?"

She closed her eyes. "Why don't you *show* me your best move?"

I let her know, "Well, I got it all planned out but I ain't perfected it just yet. Promise you won't laugh? I ain't showed the Krew yet, or even told them 'bout it. Remember the one and a half flare suicide I told you about?

Check it." I ran between two trees. I went into the one and a half forward flip and landed on both hands real solid. Then I did a airflare and transitioned to a suicide. The suicide wasn't clean, and I landed partly on my shoulder. "Ahhhh!" It scared me more than it hurt. You can break your neck messing up a suicide.

Alicia ran over. "You okay?"

I nodded. "The ground's soft. But I muffed up the suicide. Gotta land flat on your back, not on your shoulder."

I got up and rubbed the dirt off my shirt. We walked under the big trees. I grabbed Alicia's hand. "Don't tell the Krew 'bout that move. I'm keeping it on the low for now."

She kind of rolled her eyes. "Don't worry."

I tried to explain. "A b-boy's best move, the move he takes out the comp with, is called his perfection."

"Can we talk about something else?"

I nodded my head. "Okay. Can I ask you something?" Alicia nodded back. I asked her something that bothered me ever since Mr. K talked to me after class that time. "You think I'll be a loser or a bum when I grow up? Tell me for real."

She shook her head and sort of smiled like I made a joke or something. "Is there any guy at Jefferson you think I couldn't get?"

That question kind of throwed me. "No. Why?"

"You think I'd be with you if I thought you were a zero?"

I rolled my shoulders up. I asked her, "You ever think about getting out of B-town?"

"What's wrong with B-town?"

"Wouldn't it be cool to be someplace big where not everybody knows all about your business and your crew and your family and your girl?"

I pulled her to me and scoped her shiny brown eyes. We kissed and I could feel her body get bigger and smaller each time she breathed in and out. Leesha says not to kiss and tell, so keep it on the low.

BREAKBEAT 8
BACK IN THE DAY

Far as practice went, all that next week the Krew really got down. And we didn't just get down at the masonry yard. We practiced all around town. The up-est place we found was on the roof of a building where you could see the Port of Beaumont and even the refinery where Earl worked.

We went up there on a Friday after five so no one would find us. Trick had brought a big square of cardboard and a bigger square of linoleum. You put the cardboard down first so it's soft, even with all the rooftop gravel. Then you put the linoleum over the cardboard. With a linoleum surface you can really glide and spin. Big Vance had brought his boom box, and the three of us started to break things down. We really got into it for near 'bout a hour.

Then up popped two swoll cookie cops. I mean, they were just fat old security guys and not real police with guns and stuff. They came up on the roof while Trick was in the middle of a tight headspin. Trick finished up the headspin and saw them. He grabbed the boom box and ran and jumped like ten or twelve feet to the roof of the next building. I figured if Trick could do it with the box, I should be able to without.

I backed up and ran for it. I jumped and landed a whole gang of feet past the edge of the next roof. Trick shouted, "You should go out for the track team, dog!"

The cookie cops were way confused about the whole thing and started going after Vance. V looked real worried about jumping and I thought he'd get caught by them two swollers. But at the last second V ran for it and made it with a foot to spare. But he started to fall backwards off the roof. We were ten stories up. It could have been bad. Real bad. Lucky for V, me and Trick was there to grab on to him. And like I told you, Vance is dang swoll too. No featherweight.

Once Vance was safe, all three of us pointed at the cookie cops and laughed real hard. Then we hoofed it down a fire escape. The two geezers had their panties in a bunch, but there was nothing they could do. They were too old to try and jump ten feet across buildings like we did. Usually it's old people who get to have their way and their say. But that time we kids got our way. They probably just went to get doughnuts, which is what I heard real police like to do all the time too.

No one wanted to go home just yet. So we rolled to Walnut Creek to go for a dip before the sun went down. The water in Walnut Creek's too cold most the time. But that day it was just right.

After some swimming we chilled in our boxers and busted up black walnuts on the rocks. There used to be a orchard there too. Walnuts, not limes. You could eat the raw nuts. But they were bitter. And none of us really liked them too much. Still, it was fun to bust them open on the rocks.

We schemed on how all three of us could stack the paper we'd need to get to Houston and enter the Throw Down. Everybody kind of thought Mr. Bilcox would be able to take us. Big Vance asked Trick about it. Trick spit out walnut shell. "He gotta see the doc that weekend."

Big Vance turned to me. "What about *your* dad?"

I put down, "Yeah, that's a good one." Everyone in the Krew knew how my dad didn't even know 'bout me being in the Krew and all. Being part of the Krew was what I was most proud of. But Dad was too old to get it. Like how those cookie cops were too old to jump them roofs. I told Vance, "We just gotta save up bus money."

Trick reminded us, "Plus, entry's fifteen each."

Vance chimed in, "And how we gonna get from the H-town bus stop to Fifth Ward?"

Trick was like, "My boy Lester from Port Arthur can take us—we all pitch in one-twanky total. That's same as the bus, and that's to the door."

Big Vance shook his head. "DJ-screw that. What a gyp. Why he wanna charge full Greyhound prices for that limp slab he tippin'?"

Trick jumped in. "Listen up, y'all. I got a boss idea for a new dance surface."

"Yeah?" I asked.

He nodded. "Put four of them double-wide plywoods together, varnish it, and we got a real surface." Shyeah! Mr. Bilcox had a gang of plywood kicking around the masonry yard. I figured it was one of the tightest ideas for the Krew that Trick or anyone ever had.

Vance scoped to the right with a "Yo, don't look now," which of course me and Trick did. We all three watched Ruina walk over the little hill from the West and come our way.

Before Ruina could hear us, Trick put down, "He

wants back in with the Krew, and he ain't taking no for a answer. What we do?"

Vance was all, "He wants to play, he gots to pay."

What we did next, I still feel a little bad about. Even though Ruina didn't get hurt too bad. Plus, he sort of had it coming. Before we stepped into the shallows of Walnut Creek, I thought back on how everyone got started in the Krew. Trick and Vance had been best friends growing up. And they were breaking at LBJ all the way back in seventh grade.

A year later Ruina wanted to join up. They told him he had to jump out a second-story window into the prickly pear bushes before they'd even give him a shot at battling his way in. Most b-boy crews just make you battle your way in. That's where you go head to head on the floor with the best dancers on the crew. To join a crew it's usually pretty much all about your skills and attitude on the floor. Trick told me they never really meant for Ru to jump. That was just him and Vance's way of getting Ru off their backs, since they didn't think his dance skills were up to snuff back then. But Ru did jump. So Trick and Vance sort of felt like they had to let him in.

Ru was so scraped up by them thorns that he was let off school for a month. So in a way the jump was X-times-a-factor-of-two lucky for him. The principal kept asking

Ruina why he did it and Ru always said he just fell out the window by accident. With Ru in the crew, it became the Krush Krew Trio. From then on they pretty much figured anyone who wanted in would also have to go through a test first. Then get the chance to battle their way in. Sort of like how gangs make you walk the line and take a beat-down from everybody who's a member. Only the Krew tests weren't so mean or rough as all that.

In junior high two more guys tried to join the Krew. One was a skinny kid named Jimmy John Jackson. They told him to jump off a train bridge into the shallows of the creek near Old Man Owen's place. But he wouldn't do it. He probably wasn't too good a dancer anyway. The other guy was pretty swoll and went by the nickname Goose. I couldn't tell you why. They gave him the same test as Jimmy John. But Goose actually made the jump. Then Trick had him battle Ru and Big V. Goose's uprock was good. And his popping and locking was real real good. But he didn't have any power moves. Or even any groundwork at all. Poppers and lockers are pretty much one-on-one types. Crews need guys with power moves.

I started up breaking my first year at Jefferson. Trick, Vance, and Ruina had to think up a diff way to test me. The creek bed had dried up and there isn't even a single prickly pear bush at Jefferson. They decided I should pick a fight with Bobby Hanks. He was a junior and the biggest bully at Jefferson. The deal was I'd have to beat Bobby up all by myself that first fight. If I beat him that once then the Krew would always have my back against him. And anyone else at school. No matter what. Whether or not I battled my way into the Krew after that or not.

I had a idea about the best way to beat Bobby Hanks. At first I felt a little scared. But mostly I just felt amped. And if I passed the Bobby Hanks test, the dance battle part would be a gimme. At least that's what I thought. Anyway, Bobby Hanks had picked on me three or four times that September, so he had it coming. I waited till after school one day 'cause I knew he'd mess with some other freshman, like always. I saw him pushing around Ray Ray Spall, who was pretty swoll for a freshman. I snuck up behind Bobby and clocked him upside his head from behind. I gave it everything I had. Which really was none too much since I was a lot more skinny back then. Bobby turned and swung. He missed. Ray Ray picked a stick up off the ground. He smacked Bobby on the right side of his head.

Bobby fell down. He started crying like a baby. Begging us not to hurt him. Me and Ray Ray walked away from it.

But a lot of the freshmen took that chance to beat on Bobby, who'd beat on them so many times before. I guess most people who get beat on feel a lot better when they get the chance to do it back. 'Specially to the guy who did it to them.

The Krush Krew Trio debated about if it was okay that Ray Ray Spall pitched in against Bobby. But 'cause I never asked for his help, even if I thought he would help, they decided it had to count as legit. Next I had to battle my way in on the dance floor. Trick put me up against Vance. Then Ruina. Trick pretty much thought I was as good or better than the both of them. Even if he didn't say it out loud. Last but not least they had to debate about if the new name would be the Krush Krew Four or just the Krush Krew. Krush Krew is what they went with since no one knew if there might someday be a number five in the crew. Or even a number six. Dang. That would of been a lot of name changing.

Getting back to where I left off about Walnut Creek. At first Ruina wasn't sure what he'd have to do to be a part of the Krew again. Me and Trick and Big Vance made a triangle in the shallows. Mr. Kaprinski would have called it a equilateral triangle. Ruina got out in the middle wearing nothing but his dirty tightie-whities. He had even took the little feather earring out of his left ear. The tightie-whities were wet from the cold water, and you could see Ru's pickle all shriveled up. Not like I really scoped it up close or something. And, not to floss, but I think mines was like twice the size of Ru's. Even when it was 100 percent asleep. But maybe it was just the ice cold river water. You know how that works.

Ru was all, "Which one of you biz-natches gonna start this?"

Vance made a fist and got all bowed up. "Come git some, clown."

But I got this little jolt inside. Like a shock from somewhere in my gut. I wanted to be the one to tag Ruina before anyone. I told Vance, "Hold up. I want first lick." I could see Ruina, Trick, and Vance were all surprised. I'm usually not the first in the Krew to get physical.

Ruina held up his chin and came toward me. I pictured my brother Earl and hauled off. I drove my fist square at Ruina's nose with everything I had. It felt good to hit someone that hard. Even if I shouldn't of, 'cause he had been part of the Krew and all. Blood squirted out his nose and he fell back into the river.

Vance jumped up in the water. "Dang, Kid! You tagged him good!"

Even though I hit him with everything I had, Ruina got right up. He made his way to Trick. He stumbled. Blood trickled down from his nose to his face and chest.

Trick told him, "Wipe that crud off your face."

Ru leaned over and splashed water on his bloody face. He scoped Trick straight in the eye and asked him, "What you got, son?" Trick gave Ru a undercut to the gut. That was friendly when you think about how bad Ru's nose was bleeding.

Ru about fell. But he kept his balance. He stumbled to Vance. Vance connected a hard right to the side of his head. Ru spun. He landed face-first in the river. His body floated downstream like a log. It's funny, but just then I noticed how dark his skin was on his arms. And how light it was everywhere else.

I ran over and pulled Ru's face up out the water. "Ru! Jeez!" I told Trick and Vance he wasn't breathing. Just when they came over, Ru opened his eyes. He squirted water right into my face. Everybody laughed. Ru was faking the whole time he'd been face-down in the water. And he really had us fooled. Plus, after he took the beat-down like a soldier, we had to let him into the Krew again.

The thing about Ru you'd never know just kicking it with him is how he's got way more book smarts than the rest of the Krew put together. He took one of them number two pencil bubble-in tests freshman year and they bumped him up from regular classes to a bunch of geek honors classes and whatnot. He was doing okay and all but missed his boys. He played so stupid they dropped him all the way down to dummy classes with me and Vance. Poor old Trick was stuck pretty much by hisself in regular classes.

One time the career counselor, Mr. Molina, told me if Ru worked hard enough he could get a full scholarship to Harvard. Molina also said me and the Krew "provide him with a negative influence." So? Whoever them Harvard guys are can't be as good as the Aggies or the Horns. They never even had a TV game so far as I seen. Besides, if Molina had his facts right he'd know Ru couldn't even play touch football let alone the real thing.

That very Saturday the whole Krew, including Ru, got up early and met over at Mr. Bilcox's masonry yard. We were amped to get a new dance surface happening. And Mr. B was even there too. He pretty much told us what to do and we did it. "Sand this board." "Clamp that down here." "Varnish that section over there." You get what I'm saying.

We had lunch. Then went back to Walnut Creek to

wait for the varnish to dry. But none of us could even have too much fun there. All we could think about was trying out the new surface. Mr. Bilcox said we had to wait three or more hours. But it was only two and a half hours from when we'd put the varnish on before we had to try it.

Trick was first out. The rest of us scrambled to go next. Ru got Big V in a half nelson. I ducked under them and jumped on deck. Having that surface made my windmills flow smoother than ever. Big Vance was up next with some power moves. Then Ru, even though his nose was still swoll and puffy from the smackdown we gave him in Walnut Creek. Ru was just finishing up his set when Magno Clique rolled up in the El C. Before the slab even stopped, Vance had his hands on two bricks.

Thumping screwed and chopped, Magno Clique tipped the El C all the way up to the curb. The Clique jumped out the Camino and Warren was all, "What it do, y'all?"

I was like, "Professional chillin'. Like Kool-Aid in a cup."

Everybody from Magno peeped the new dance surface. Dap nodded his head. "Y'all be stepping your game up."

Izzle was impressed too. "That surface be funkizzle, mane." He pulled out a Swisher blunt and blazed up.

Trick got serious. "Yo, Izzle. Put out that shizzle. Y'at my daddy's place of business."

"My bizzle." Izzle dropped the blunt.

Peanut looked good. No bandages no more. He chimed in, "Yo, 'fore we rock this, y'all know what my brother Pedro told me that Ruina's cousin Miguel told him?" The Krew waited to hear what Peanut had to say. "He said y'all need wheels to H-town like bad."

"Oh really?" I asked.

Ru shook his head. "Pedro wouldn't of told you jack."

Peanut asked, "Then how I know what I know?"

From the look on Ru's face I could tell his cousin Miguel was in for a *familia*-style beatdown if it was true. I mean, if he'd been talking with the Clique about the Krew. Even if it was in a good way.

"What's it to y'all how we get to H-town?" I wanted to know.

Peanut stepped in all sly-like. "You know we hitting the Throw Down that weekend. Like that's how it is anyway. So we got room if y'all wanna tip Magno Clique style."

Trick peeped the El Camino bed. It had two twanky-inch woofers bolted in. "Six mugs in back, plus them woofers?"

Dap pointed. "Three up front, five in back, and if y'all tippin' with us, I'll yank them woofers."

I wanted to know, "How much paper we gotta drop?"

Dap was like, "Fitty-fitty on gas. 'Cause like P said, we tippin' there any which way you dice it."

Just then, Big Vance pushed play on his box and got a speeded-up beat thumping. "Y'all donkey dongs come to rap or battle?"

Warren stepped to the box. "Hold up." He ejected Trick's mix tape from Vance's box. He took the tape over to the slab and popped it into the deck in Dap's El C. That got things thumping bigtime. As much of the foolio as Warren could act, sometimes you had to give him props.

BREAKBEAT 9
TOE TO TOE WITH MAGNO

There was a bunch of stress around the cypher 'cause of how V had knocked out Peanut and all. But everybody in the Krew and the Clique fronted like it wasn't nothin' but a thang. I mean, we were ready to get into it and really mix it up on the battle tip. Vance stepped up first. In crew-on-crew street battles there's no law saying which crew, or which b-boy, goes first. Someone just steps into the cypher and throws down. The only real rule is that crews take turns. First one, then the other. And most crews save their strongest weapons for last. Or at least hardly never send them in first. No offense, V. Before Vance hit the deck he got into some uprock. His footwork was real fancy. But the best thing was how he got in Peanut's grill with some Sammo Hung kung fu–type hand moves.

Sammo's that swoll Chinaman in the first battle against Bruce Lee in *Enter the Dragon*. A few times it seemed like V was gonna for sure hit Peanut. Which might have meant a real rumble like in back of the school that time. But close as he got, V never even touched Peanut. Just like how it should be in a b-boy battle. With no one getting hurt or even contacted. I was surprised how Peanut never blinked even once during V's uprock. Dang. A straight up no-blink machine.

Next Vance hit the ground for a turtle and handglide combo. But it turned out to be a icy-ice and handglide combo. A turtle's where you're face-down, with only your hands touching the deck. Then you go around and around in a circle like a umbrella being twirled around with its handle on the ground. A icy-ice is basically a turtle. But with your head on the deck. So it's easier than a turtle but still pretty dope. Vance comboed from the icy-ice to a handglide. That's pretty much like it sounds. The combo part means he went smooth from the one move to the next. The glide part's about sliding over the ground with whatever part of your body. Trick can even do headslides like a mug. But I'll get to that later.

Next, Vance did some six-step—that downrock move I told about before. Where you're on your hands and feet, basically kicking around in a circle on the floor. Then he broke into some bellymills. Me, Trick, and Ru all high-fived and were like, "Hells shyeah!" Vance was the only one in the Krew who could do bellymills. Basically, they're upturned windmills. You could see by the look on Peanut's face he was sweating Vance's set. And you couldn't fault him. Anyway, with bellymills your legs stay spread out in a V shape. You rotate real smooth from your belly to your back, and keep repeating. Staying smooth is key. Any wiggedy-whack punk can flip from his belly to his back. But making it flow, with your legs to keep the rotations going smooth, is what it's all about. Vance was out of breath. But the whole Krew booty-slapped him when he wrapped his set. Trick was like, "Way to put that swolled-up belly to use!" And Vance was so stoked he even laughed at Trick's fat-boy joke. Instead of getting red in the face like sometimes.

Peanut stepped into the cypher with some solid up-rock. Then he hit the deck. Peanut and Vance had their animosity meters up in the red zone 'cause of how Vance threw down on P in back of the school. So I knew the set would be as off the chain as P could make it. After a few circles of six-step Peanut changed his game up with a boomerang. You're still doing circles with the boomerang. Start with your booty on the ground, legs in front of you in a V shape. Use your hands to lift off the ground. Then turn 'round and 'round with nothing but your hands on deck. The quicker the better. And Peanut was pretty dang quick. Vance fronted like he didn't even notice. But of course we all did.

Peanut threw down a bunch of turtles. Which was kind of him dissin' on Vance's icy-ices. I already told you they're almost the same but easier. Peanut went for the finish line with a cricket-jackhammer combo. A cricket's basically a hyped-up turtle. And a jackhammer's basically a hyped-up cricket. With crickets you not only rotate around on the deck in a circle using your hands like in a turtle, you also jump up and down on your hands.

It's easy to lose balance and face-plant. But I gotta admit, Peanut held it down. He went from crickets to jackhammers. They're pretty much like crickets. 'Cept instead of bouncing up and down and rotating in a circle on both hands, you can only use one. Done right, it's a sick move. And Peanut didn't even flub it once. The whole Krew felt bad for Vance that Peanut did so good. He closed with a flip onto his back and grabbed his nutsack in V's direction and told him, "Bite me, biz-natch!"

That wasn't cool of Peanut. But so long as you don't touch your opponent, pretty much anything goes in the cypher. It's your time to shine. Still, I knew it took everything Vance had to not jump P for that one. I peeped Trick and could tell he was frettin' on Vance, same as me. You know how when you look at your illest friend and know they're thinking the same thing as you. But lucky for everyone, V kept his cool. Sort of. I heard him mumble something under his breath about "cracking a Peanut next time" or something like that. Magno got the idea but kept it chill. You had to hand it to them. They could hold it down and stay in control no matter how hard you tried to mess with their heads. Then V did a farmer's blow. That's where you blow your nose into the air without a hanky or anything. A fat green loog flew out of V's nose and accidentally hit Ruina's leg. Poor Ru. The whole Magno Clique cracked up and pointed at where the loog stuck to Ru's leg. Ru was all amped and set to punch Vance's mug. But he just shook his head, stooped down, and wiped it off with some dried-up oak leaves.

Izzle stepped into the cypher, still laughing at Ru. I looked at Ru, who should of been on deck 'cause him and Izzle always squared off. In a judged battle you hardly never see two guys from the same crew go one behind the other. But street battles are diff. And a lot more goes. Izzle must of went first to try and mess with Ru's head. But he was chill as a popsicle. Izzle dropped right into some helicopters. You squat on one leg, stretch the other leg out, then move it around and around in a circle like a helicopter blade. The tricky part's timing it so the squatting leg can jump the blade leg when it goes under you. Next Izzle threw down genies. They're windmills, 'cept with your hands crossed in front of your chest. It's harder than your everyday windmill since you can't use your hands for power or balance. Izzle changed his game up by switching from genies to handcuffs.

Handcuffs are also a kind of windmill. But you have your hands behind your back, like you been shackled by the police. They're even more hard than genies 'cause you gotta watch out, on top of everything else, that you don't roll on your hands. After two rotations Izzle lost his juice. On the third rotation he came to a sloppy stop and tried to front like it was freeze. He scoped Ru and was all, "I W-to-tha-izzill bet good paper, ya wiznack whack punk bizz-uger izass can't top thiznat." Izzle always made smack-talking part of his game in the cypher. Which pretty much tells you how shaky the kid was about his moves.

Ruina stepped into the cypher. He got in Izzle's grill

with some clownin' and krumpin' shakes. Then some lockin' and poppin'. It was sweet to have Ru back reppin' the Krew in the cypher after basically a year away in Cali. And it was double sweet how his L.A. stylins threw the whole Clique off. You could scope it in their faces. Ru laid down his own set of helicopters. They were way tighter than Izzle's. Next he worked in some applejacks. You squat on both legs, then fall back on your hands and kick one leg up so high your foot goes past your head. Ru jumped up from his applejacks, ran forward, and did a gainer. That's where you run forward, then do a full backwards flip. Cross your fingers for good luck and hope you land on your feet and not on your head or your booty. Ru closed out with some perfect nutcrackers. You know, those windmills where you hold your tallywhacker. Hopefully for Ru his Vienna sausage had got unshriveled from how it was back at Walnut Creek.

Ru spun around and around like a loco top. He came to a stone cold freeze. The whole Krew was hyped. Izzle shook his head and you could hear him talking to the Clique under his breath. "That clizzown got some serious krizzump in his trizunk." Coming from Izzle that was pretty swoll props.

Trick was so amped, he busted into the cypher next.

Officially it should have been someone from the Clique on deck. But 'cause of what Izzle had pulled, the Clique pretty much owed us one. Trick's first move was a Colt 45. It's a James Brown move where you kick a leg forward and bring it back behind the other knee. Then bend that second knee forward and drop to the floor. Pop back up and do it all over again. It's a mega-ol'-skool move. But Trick's style made it look fresh. One old-timer told me J.B. was the hardest grinding man in show biz. And the original hip-hop head, way before even DJ Kool Herc. Like, at least since 1968 when Hotlanta's own dropped "Say It Loud—I'm Black and I'm Proud." That year changed the world. Me and the Krew still break to that track.

Trick followed with a bunch of eggbeaters. Basically windmills where your hands are way high up on your hips. After spinning out a few eggbeaters he moved to T-flares. That takes mad skill. Even basic flares ain't a gag. It's kind of like windmills since your legs are more high in the air than anything else. And your legs do circle after circle like in a windmill. But instead of rotating on the ground from shoulder to shoulder, with flares you transfer the rotation and weight from hand to hand.

If you ever seen the Olympics, there's these fruity gymnastic guys in tights. They get on a little bench called a horse that gots handles on top of it. They start spinning around with just their hands, legs swinging up from side to side and circling in the air and around them. That's what flares are like. 'Cept with flares you just got the ground to work with. There's no handles and no high-up horse bench thing to keep your legs from hitting the deck when you rotate. Them Olympics guys got nothing on b-boy flares. Specially T-flares. With T-flares you gotta keep your legs real tight together. With everyday flares you can have your legs spaced apart a little or even a lot. Trick closed out with a pretzel-looking freeze.

Like I already said, Dap's the Clique's mackest dancer. And since Trick's pretty much the Krew's best, 'cept maybe me on my good days, Dap glided into the cypher next. He did some poplock that put Michael Jackson's ol'-skool-type moonwalking to shame. Then he busted out a few Colt 45s. He yawned while he did them just to mess with Trick's mind. Shyeah, right. Like that would even faze Trick. Next Dap threw down a few everyday flares. He stepped it up to airflares. A airflare's one of the most baddest b-boy skills out there. It's where your legs are way high in the air and you jump off one hand, rotate a half circle around, then land on the other hand. And it was Dap's perfection. He ended with a freeze. Dang. Me and the Krew couldn't believe that after Trick's super-tight set Dap was still able to take him out strong like that. I patted Trick on the back. Sometimes there's nothing else you can do.

Magno Clique was still celebrating when Vance pushed me into the cypher. After throwing some uprock in Warren's grill, I dropped to the deck and put down a few circles of six-step. Then a gang of tictacs. You know, them Russian-type kicks. I planned my next move to be a drill headspin. Where you go from a headstand into a spin. You use your hands to rotate and pick up speed. Then twist your legs together and straighten them up higher and higher. That makes you spin faster and faster. Kind of like how when you're on a merry-go-round and pull yourself into the middle and things spin quicker and quicker. Way back in freshman year Miss McGonagal, the old maid science teacher, called it centrafrugal force or something like that.

Anyway, like Dap, I finished with some airflares. But after two flares I couldn't rotate a full half-circle to the next hand. I landed hard on my shoulder. I played it off like I meant to do it. But everybody in the Krew and the Clique knew better. I still couldn't believe how easy Dap made airflares look. Before I could even get out of the cypher, Warren threw down some uprock in my face. Talk about a eager beaver.

Warren dropped his skinny red bones to the deck. He did a vertical pushup. Next he went into a long set of air-swipes and backswipes. Airswipes are where you flip around and around with your body horizontal to the ground. You kick your legs up with your weight on one arm. Then flip over and land on your other arm before your legs land. You've gotta go and go to make it look good. And Warren did. Backswipes are the same as air-swipes. But you reverse direction when your legs are in the air and flip back to starting position. Warren's set was so tight I couldn't stomach watching his outro. But with one scope to Trick's face I knowed Warren finished double dang good. I could see Trick felt mega shamed. Losing to your archrival is like someone knocking you to the ground and peeing on you. Really, it's even more worse than that 'cause at least you can take a shower and soap up if somebody peed on you. But there's no soap to wash out that dead feeling when you been beat down by your staunchest comp.

After the battle was all said and done, Peanut stepped to Big Vance and put his fist out. That kind of made up for dissin' Vance before with that nut-grabbing freeze.

Vance was cool 'bout it and knocked fists with Peanut. Izzle and Ru did the same. Then Trick and Dap. Which left only me and Warren. He put out his right fist. I knuckled mine against his. Even with all the bad stuff that happened before, we were able to keep it a chill and friendly neighborhood battle. Just like Izzle'd said a week before.

Magno Clique headed over to the slab and Dap was all, "So. Should I yank them woofers before Friday?" That was his way of checking to see if the Krew would be tippin' with the Clique to H-town.

Trick was like, "Already. But the Throw Down goes down Saturday."

Izzle chimed in, "Shyeah, but the plizzay's ta ciznamp Friday night."

Ru put down, "We just tippin' to H-town, not El Paso. Why we gotta camp out?"

P stepped in. "Can't speak for the Krew, but the Clique wants to hit the rec center bright and early, get warmed up."

Warren jumped in like a salesman. "Plus, camping out near the Big H means a couple hours more sleep than tippin' from B-town at the crack of dawn. You feel me?"

Me and the Krew scoped each other for a long second. T told the Clique to hold up. The Krew got into a little huddle and we all talked in whispers. Vance was like, "Who needs them? Let's bus it."

Ru looked at Trick. "I don't trust them punks."

Trick shook his head. "I ain't got a good vibe about it neither. But we could save paper. Plus it's to the front door. Kid?"

I don't gotta tell you again how short I was on paper. "I say we do it."

Ru was about ready to hit me. "Funk that, Kid. They fittin' to jack us, mane."

I full on grinned at Ru like I was about to make a gag, which I half was. "Too bad your vote don't count yet, newbie." Then I scoped Trick and nodded to let him know I was serious about tippin' with Magno.

Trick stood up and shouted over to Magno, "Shyeah! We'll tip with the Clique. Just don't be late."

Warren cracked a devilish grin and chunked the deuce. "Don't even stress. We on atomic clock time." The rest of the Clique chunked the deuce and jumped in the El C. Then they peeled off.

Big Vance was trying to talk to Trick about something, and Ru leaned over to me. "You made the wrong choice, Kid."

"What? Letting your skeezin' ass back into the Krew?"

"You know what I mean. You can't trust nobody from Magno."

There was a question I'd been meaning to ask Ru ever since he got back. "That sponsor out in Cali. How much you get paid?"

"Two Gs."

"A week?"

"Nah, Kid. A month."

"What went down, clown?"

Ru rolled his shoulders up. "Guess they didn't want me no more."

B-side
BATTLE & AFTERMATH

BREAKBEAT 10
WHO GOT PAPER?

That night I stacked change. Dimes. Nickels. Even pen-
nies. All three stacks only came to $11.32. Dang it, mane.
Me and Trick figured it would be at least ten bones each
for gas roundtrip. Eight for food if we ate careful. Then
the fifteen-dollar entry fee. That meant we needed at least
thirty-three green ones each. I was basically twanky-two
short. And there was only one person I could figure to
ask. I knocked on Earl's door. I heard him scooch back
from his desk and pad across the room. He opened the
door smoking one of Dad's Winstons. I could see some
kind of electronics manual on his lit-up desk. He must
have been boning up when I knocked. Earl knew a lot
about electronics and mechanics and stuff like that and
was always reading up more on it.

"Yo, Earl."

"Yo, what?"

"I was gonna ask you something."

"Ask." Earl could be point blank like that.

"Well. I was gonna ask you could I borrow, like, twanky—uh, twenty-two dollars."

Earl took in a puff of smoke. He blew it right in my face. "Like, uh, get a job." He started to shut the door.

I blocked it with my left foot. "I'll pay you back. It's for the weekend. The dance-off."

"Ask Dad."

I looked at my feet and didn't have a comeback.

But Earl thought he had a comeback to his own comment and he kept on. "You know damn well he'd be ashamed. Paying green money to twitch your backside around like some jigaboo."

I heard my voice break. "Twenty-six dollars, Earl. I'll wash your clothes and clean your room. For a month." And I meant it too.

Earl picked at his nose. "I already got someone doing that for me."

I was like, "Yeah, and maybe you don't want Dad knowing who it is . . ."

He opened the door up wider and stepped to me. He

jabbed at me with two fingers and the lit cigarette. "Tell him whatever you want. And get set for consequences." Then he slammed the door in my face. Dang. If the Guinness book had a stankhole competition, I'd put all my paper and change on Earl. Then again, my problem was not having the chips to place a bet any which way in the first place. Pawning Moms's diamond wedding ring was one idea for Throw Down paper that popped into my head. But it wasn't right. And I wasn't gonna do it. Not unless it was the one and only way.

If me and the Krew wanted to go the distance we'd have to prep to rep B-town to the hip-hop nation. For the next two weeks I trained like a mug. Chin-ups in the lime grove. Racing my bike against all the hazardous materials freight trains rolling East to Livonia. Swimming upstream in Walnut Creek. And doing the one and a half to a flare suicide time and again. I was real scared about suiciding onto hard ground. So I only did it on the soft dirt at the lime grove. Or into the water at Walnut Creek.

'Bout a week after the Fourth of July, me and Alicia were pro chilling by her locker. She reminded me how her cousin Clarita's *quinceañera* was coming up later that week and all. Dang. So it was going down the very same Saturday as the Throw Down. Alicia was none too happy to hear I couldn't be her *quinceañera* date since I'd already told her I could. Her locker was open to where you could see the pictures she'd pasted in there of me and her. We got the pictures from one of them black-and-white photo booths. You know the kind. Anyway, Alicia kind of shoved me back. "What you mean you can't come to the *quinceañera* with me? I already told my whole *familia* you'd be with me."

"Yeah, but I didn't know it was going down the same Saturday as the Throw Down."

"Kid. I *told* you when it was when I *invited* you. Besides, what's the big deal about the Throw Down?"

I had to cold correct her. "What's the big deal? If me and the Krew even make the semifinals, we'll be the first crew in *history* to put B-town on the map."

I wanted her to understand how me being a b-boy meant everything. I wanted to tell her it was the only thing I was ever any good at. But I couldn't figure how to say it. While I was thinking of what to say I leaned in and tried to *béseme* her. That's Mexican for muggin' down. But she leaned back on her locker, pushed me away, and rolled her eyes at me. "Stop."

Her pushing me off like that threw me a bit. I asked her what it did.

She scoped the floor. "Look, Kid. I got a confession. I can't handle Clarita. Or her sisters. That's why you gotta come."

That threw me even more and I told her, "I don't get it."

"My aunt and uncle spoil them like three little *princesas*. They get whatever they want and always rub my nose in it. Clarita told me her dad's gonna throw the *quinceañera* and buy her a brand-new Volkswagen. Big deal."

"Yeah? And? Why you steamed if I can't go?"

Leesha got shy and scoped the ground. "You'll laugh."

"No I won't. Go ahead. I promise."

She looked up at me. "The only reason I even wanna go is to show you off. To my cousins. To my grandma. My aunts. My uncles. Everyone. At least I got one thing Clarita will never have."

I gave Alicia a little grin so she'd know I was just gagging. I asked her, "How you know that? Is she hot? I mean, *caliente*?"

"Kid. I'm serious."

"I don't know what to say. Me and the Krew been practicing like mugs all summer for the Throw Down. I can't dog my boys like that."

She got sad and mad at one and the same time. "Okay.

I got it. You care less about me than those *pendejo* losers you call friends."

Her dissin' on the Krew like that stoked my steam meter up to 100. I wanted to smack someone. Hard enough to put a hurt on them. But I couldn't hit her 'cause she was a girl. Plus, she wasn't just any old bopper, but my girl on top of it all. So I punched her locker. Pretty hard too. I skinned most my right-hand knuckles. "What's your problem, Leesha? Don't ever talk about the Krew like that. Never."

She still had her attitude and was all, "Oh, but it's okay for you to talk about my girl Teresa like that."

"That trick? Don't make me laugh."

"Whatever, Paul Wall Junior."

It got to me. I pushed her without even thinking before I did it. I told her, "Go do yourself."

"Eat me." She started to walk away like she didn't even give a flying F.

I asked her to hold up.

She threw back, "You need to learn respect."

I couldn't even look at her. I felt pretty off for getting steamed at her and all. Plus, it's hard to ask for help when you just lost it on somebody. I talked to her all quiet-like and polite. But I don't think she knew I meant it. "I'm sorry, Leesha. Hey, I was thinking 'bout asking you . . . could I borrow like maybe twanky dollars?" It was harder asking her than Earl. 'Specially since I'd just pushed her and all.

"How come?"

"It's . . . it's so I can tip to the Throw Down with the Krew."

"Borrow it from your crew boyfriends, since they're so great." She slammed her locker shut. She walked away without even turning back once to see if I was watching her. Which of course I was. She'd told me a few times before that her moms had mad stacks tucked away here and there. Why couldn't Leesha just front me the paper?

I called out after her. "Yo, Leesha. Can't you get it? That's who I am." All the other kids in the hall turned and scoped me like they thought I was smoking wacky tabacky. It felt like one of them dreams where you think you're naked at school. 'Cept it wasn't a dream. And I had my clothes on.

That night after Lori went out shopping, I slinked into her and Dad's room. He was passed out with a quarter-full bottle of J.T.S. Brown next to his head. Like a pillow. I thought about taking a nip just for giggles. But I didn't.

I crept over to the closet by tiptoe. The door creaked a little when I opened it. But not so much as to wake Dad. It took me no time flat to find the orange shoebox. I knew right where it was.

I snuck the shoebox into my room and opened it. It was full up with lots of old pictures and ticket stubs and stuff like that. I fished around and pulled out a empty orange plastic doctor's bottle. It said, *"Geraldine Kirwin— take 1 pill by mouth nightly as sleep aid if needed—Seconal."* A little sticker on the bottle said, *"Keep out of reach of children."* I had a pretty good notion why Dad kept the bottle. But I didn't really want to think on it.

I dug around the bottom and pulled out what I was looking for. A big diamond ring all set in gold. It was Moms's wedding ring before she died. It really shined. I pocketed the ring and grabbed out one of the old pictures from the shoebox.

It was real faded and showed the family. With my real moms and no Lori. We were standing outside the house. The house was a lot nicer in the picture. And Moms was twanky-something or other and wore a purple sweater. In that picture she kind of reminded me of me. Everyone had full on smiles. 'Cept Earl, who'd gave me bunny ears and had stuck his tongue out at the camera. Mane, I guess some people can be like that their whole life. Pass the word on to the folks at Guinness about Earl acting the stankhole fool even way back then. 'Cause once I do got them chips, I'm gonna place that bet.

Another picture showed me when I was still in diapers. Dad was on his back. He held me straight up in the air. No matter how big or strong I could ever get, I'd never be able to hold him up like he held me in that picture. You could tell he was a proud papa 'cause he was grinning like all get out. You couldn't blame him. Since, on the real, I was pretty dang cute. Now he never even gave you a pat on the back anymore. Plus, me, Dad, and Earl didn't even punch each other on the shoulders like we did back in the day. I patted my pocket to make sure the ring was still tucked safe in there. I took one more look at my real moms in the first picture. And I told her, "I'm just lending it, Ma."

Mr. Larson's door made that same Christmas jingle like before. The old man turned around. "You got something digital for me?"

I fished into my pocket. "Nah. I got a diamond ring . . . and gold."

"Where you get it?"

I handed the ring to him. He held it up to the light and let loose with a loud laugh. And it seemed like he was sort of laughing at me.

"What's so funny?"

"Band's gold all right. Fourteen carat. But this ain't no diamond."

"You're wrong," I told him point blank.

"Am I really? I suppose you the world expert on cubic zirconium."

"But it can't be. It's my moms's . . . it's a wedding ring. From a real wedding."

"I don't care if it's from a crackerjack box or a French museum. The stone be phony."

"But it can't be" was the only thing I could say, all over again.

He rolled his shoulders up and held the ring back out to me. "Take it over the state line to Zillers, you don't believe me."

"How . . . how much?"

"I give you thirty."

"Thirty dollars? That's all?"

I only needed twanky-six. I asked him, "How long you can hold it?"

"A month. At twenty-five percent interest."

I did the math out loud. "X times point-two-five equals . . . lemme think . . . thirty-dollars . . . umm . . . that's seven dollars fifty?"

"Umm-hmm. Plus a five-dollar service charge. We gotta take that out up front." It all sounded regular so I told him to go ahead and do it. Some people give you that shiesty vibe like you better watch your back or they'll dog you. I could tell right off with Mr. Larson it wasn't like that.

In gym class they tell you not to practice too much the day before a game. But that night before we tipped to H-town, I couldn't help but bust out a gang of airtwists, drill headspins, and airflares in my bedroom. For a good two hours. The airflares were too hard and I couldn't really do them up to perfection. Next day when we met up over at Bilcox Masonry, I wasn't the only one sore as a chilly mo.

Big V dug through a big ol' yellow backpack trying to find a candy bar.

Ru shook his head. "S'already seven-ten. They most definitely giving us the dodge."

Trick spat at the ground. "Didn't I tell you they was pulling stunts, Kid? Huh?"

Big Vance stood up. "Last night bus to H-town left a half a hour ago."

Ru rolled his shoulders up. "Nothing going in the a.m. We don't hot-wire a slab tonight, we gonna miss the Throw Down."

Trick got up in my grill. "Told you tippin' with Magno was a dumb idea."

I told Trick, "Bull you did. You and me both figured it was the best thing."

Big V pushed me. "Trick wouldn't of been down if you didn't chime in. Lame brain."

Now it was on. If Vance could push, so could I. I pushed him back hard and told him to step off. Big V bounced back at me. He tried a roundhouse but missed. Then Ru and Trick jumped into the mix. Pretty soon everybody was yelling at everybody. Then all of a sudden there was a loud honk. We turned and saw the El C. Everybody in the Krew shut up. Dap was thumping screw and sittin' sideways. He grinned over at us. "What it do, Krush Krew?" Everybody in Magno Clique busted up laughing. Then the Krew started chuckling too.

I patted Trick on the back. "Told you they'd be here."

By the time we were rolling over Peterson Bayou the sun was set to set. Dap had the El C cruising 'bout seventy-five on the speedometer. But it was a old slab and I bet we were really tippin' more like eighty or eighty-five. I'd say Dap was rolling that fast to see when somebody in the Krew would stress and bellyache about it. But none of us did. The Krew could be straight up soldiers. Most 'specially when someone was stress testing us like that.

Warren rode shotgun and Ruina rode *chica* in the middle of the front seat. Dap's El C had a changed-up rear window you could open. That way you could talk to whoever was riding in the bed. Which was me and Trick, Vance, Peanut, and Izzle. I never could figure if an El Camino was a pickup truck trying to be a car or a car trying to be a pickup. The bayou really whizzed past. It made me think of that time me and Earl and my moms went to New Orleans by train.

Trick piped up. "Dang. Y'all hungry?"

I told him, "Nah."

Trick was all, "Well, I ain't hungry neither, I'm *hong-gry*. I gotta munch something right quick, mane." It didn't add up. Trick had told me he'd ate a phat dinner before meeting up over at the masonry yard.

Vance held up his giant yellow backpack. "I got a boatload of chili in here."

Peanut was like, "Psss . . . chili? Who made it, *gringo*?"

Vance rolled his shoulders up. "I don't know. It's in some big ol' cans from out my mom's cupboard. We going camping, so let's heat it up on a campfire. And, yo, check out the leftovers from the Fourth."

V pulled out three roman candles from his pack and shouted at Dap. "Stop!"

Dap screeched the slab to a full stop. "What the hell?"

Big V held up the three candles. "Too much wind." He lit all three at once and aimed them at the bayou. Dap shook his head and got the slab tippin' again. You could hear the fireballs crackle every time they hit water. It wasn't but a half minute and all three candles were done.

Peanut scoped the bayou. The sun sank down into it without even a sizzle. Peanut was all, "They say lots of mugs get buried in the bayou and they don't never find them."

I wanted to know, "Then how they know that's where they buried in the first place?"

"I don't know. That's just what they say."

I got a funny vibe. I didn't want to think about if maybe there was dead people rotting out there in the bayou. Like that mule under the lime tree I saw way back. I felt better as soon as we got off the bayou.

Up in front Ru painted Vogue yellow krump paint on his face. Then he used the paint stick to tag his name graffiti-style on his left shoulder. Most Third Coast b-boys respect what krumpers and clowners did for L.A. But hardly none slap war paint on before a battle. Dap hit a bump going over eighty. But Ruina stayed in control of the paint stick.

Dap checked Ru and shook his head. "That's a fruity tat, Ru." Ru just ignored him.

Then Dap felt up his wood steering wheel like it was a bopper or something. "Yo, check this wood grain."

Ru asked, "Is it *pecker*wood?"

Dap pretend laughed. "Har har har."

Trick spotted a fast food billboard and asked to stop. But Vance reminded him 'bout the chili.

Then Ru got all abstract and whatnot. "I'll give y'all one guess as to the difference between tagging and advertising." None of us had a idea what Ru was getting at, so he laid it out. "Paper, pure and simple. And don't quote me. That's my boy Crüz from H-town dropping science. Say a fast food company wants to get in your grill to pimp their burgers and fries. They don't gotta ask your personal permission. They just gotta drop some change on some cat who controls a billboard and that's their permission. Taggers, we just bomb the message we want, and don't drop paper to do it. Shyeah." My head hurt from all the science Ru had dropped. I told you before, Ru's the book smart one in the Krew.

Vance signaled to Peanut. "Speaking of dropping, I'm 'bout to drop a new rhythm. Ready, get set, P." Then he busted out some dope human beatbox. Like a straight up ol'-skool drum machine.

Peanut nodded his head to the beat. Then he spit some freestyle in Mexican and English. "Gettin' hong-gree, so we need *alimentos*, *ochental* cans of chili, with pimentos. We tippin' El Camino style, no Pinto, to Bloody Fifth Ward, H-town, *El Quinto* . . ."

It wasn't no time and we were less than a hour East of H-town. We looked around for like a hour, scouting a place to camp. We found a pretty good spot. It seemed like a woods no one used. Dap jumped a parking lot curb onto some old dirt road. Some sign said PARK VEHICLES ONLY or whatever.

Peanut turned. "What y'all think?"

"Spooky," Trick said. And I had to agree with him.

Warren was like, "We gotta get a fire going."

It was getting dark and I asked if somebody had a flashlight.

Vance nodded. "Shyeah, in my backpack."

Izzle wanted to know, "What else you got in thizzat B to tha izzack pizzack?"

Vance got a full on grin. "Pictures of me and your kid bro tryin' to lick-us my sack-us."

With all them gay jokes Vance was always throwing down, you sometimes had to wonder. I didn't know what Izzle was gonna say. But he just busted out laughing. So we all did too. "Thata been F-U-double-nizzy. *If* I had a kid bro."

Dap put the brakes on the slab and yanked the keys from the ignition. Using Vance's flashlight, we all grabbed up some wood and started a campfire. Vance got busy pitching up a tent. But it didn't look as big as he'd said, which was that it could supposedly fit like eight or more people. Vance opened a can of chili and chucked it right on the fire. And when it was hot we all ate with some spoons I snaked the day before from the Jefferson cafeteria.

Izzle sparked up a Swisher blunt. "Any y'all trying to get twizzy on some Swizzy?"

Everybody but Dap shook their head. Warren dug around in the El C. He came back hoisting two forties. "One of these got Krush Krew's name on it fo sho." Warren handed me one of the forties. I popped the cap and took a sip. It was so strong it made me squint.

Vance put his hand out. "Gimme that, wuss-bag fag." He near guzzled a quarter of the forty in one go. He let out a nasty burp.

Peanut sipped from the other forty, then held it out

for Vance to clink. V was surprised. But he did clink bottles with Peanut.

Peanut grinned. "'Tween Magno and Krush Krew, people are gonna know 'bout B-town."

Warren nodded. "Sho nuff. This year ain't about making a name for one crew or the other."

Vance doubted on Warren. "Then what's it about?"

Warren came right back at him. "Making a name for B-town, big boy."

Dap held some smoke in. After he let it out he said, "Listen, y'all. Just 'cause the summer started off on a bad foot don't mean it can't end up on the good foot." Dap stared at the fire and took another drag off the Swisher. "Yo. Magno and the Krew should come together. Form a supercrew. Couldn't nobody stop us."

Trick looked around at Magno and shook his head. "You can't be serious."

Warren nodded. "No doubt. Four plus four. That's a eight-man crew. Why not?"

Peanut jumped in. "I'm down. What y'all say?"

Big V spit into the fire. "Not to dis, but funk that."

Ru looked across the fire at Magno. "Saying we joined up together, what would we call the supercrew?"

Warren grinned like he was about to gag. "I vote for Krush Clique."

I gagged right back. "Long as we spell Klick with a K."

Everybody from both crews chuckled it up. I guzzled most of what was left of the forty.

Izzle put his hand out. "Pass tha drizzle, wizzle."

I passed it over and scoped the fire. Then Magno. I told them, "It's a honor y'all wanna go into battle with us. But let's everybody sleep on it."

Warren nodded. "Square enough."

Izzle and Dap called the El C. Everybody else crammed into the tent. Warren squirmed. "This be cramped as a mug. I'm crashing in the slab."

Peanut was all, "Word. I heard that."

Ruina moved over. "Izzle and Dap already crashed the Camino bed."

Warren called shotgun. That would leave Peanut in the tent. Or crammed in the driver's seat with the steering wheel. I squirreled around in the tent and tried to get comfy. I pushed Vance. "I thought this was supposed to fit like eight people."

"Yeah. That's what my bro told me. Sucker's a boy scout."

Trick put down, "Zack? He a cub scout. You trusted a ten-year-old. That's some lame junk, man."

Warren unzipped the front tent flap. But Vance grabbed

him by the shoulder. "Hold up, mane. You gotta check my latest beatbox ditty."

Warren was like, "Huh?"

Brrp, brrp, brriip, brrp, brrp, brriip was the sound Vance made when he let some well-timed gas on a proper beat.

I put a shirt over my nose and talked through it. "God-dang. Nasty." Warren unzipped the tent flap the rest the way and jumped out right quick, with Peanut on his tail.

Peanut was like, "That's serious." And he wasn't lying. Peanut and Warren ran for the El C. Who could blame them?

Trick's nose sounded pinched. "Damn. Damn, that jazz be rancid. That jazz ain't right."

Big Vance was all, "It keeps the mosquitoes away."

Trick asked, "What mosquitoes?"

Vance cracked a big ol' grin. "Exactly."

I heard the doors to the El C slam shut. Then I heard some kind of rumbling. "Y'all hear that?"

Trick waved his hand over his nose. "That best not be you again, V."

Vance got stressed. "Hold up. Ain't no one from Magno up in here."

I called him out. "With that rank ass, who gonna blame them?"

Vance shook his head. "Yo, somebody from the Krew better stay up and keep a watch on them donkeys."

Trick punched Vance in the shoulder. "You go right ahead, big boy."

A while later, after Trick fell asleep, I heard a low rumble sound again. Just when I was gonna call Vance on it, I could tell it was a barred owl whooing from somewhere deep in the woods. My brother Earl taught me to recognize their sound. Back when we was still copacetic. The barred owl always asks the same question. "Whoo cooks for you? Whoo cooks for ya-all?"

I went to sleep thinking how funny it was that even a wise old owl couldn't get the answers to everything.

The whooing of the barred owl took me off to a weird sleep. I dreamed everything was black. Then bright white. Then there was a weird sound. Like a truck moving over gravel. I blinked awake. A light shined on the tent. Headlights. Before I could think, the roof of the tent came down on my face. Like it was hit down with baseball bats. I felt sticks. Something hit my face. I tried to get away. But I was caught up. In the tent. I flailed around. Trying to get out. Escape. But I was accidentally hitting Trick. Or Vance. Or Ru. And they were accidentally hitting me too.

The baseball bats or clubs or whatever kept raining down on us. Harder and harder. I recognized Peanut's voice. "Who the mane now, ya fat-butt Crisco-munching pink swoll? Huh? How you like me now?"

Next, Warren. "Lily-ass cracker-lovin-ass homos." But the baseball bat hits didn't stop.

I heard them both laughing. And the hits wouldn't stop. Then I heard Izzle. "Pizzay-back's a bee-yotch, ain't it?"

It sounded like Warren again. "Enough is enough, y'all. They out like the vapors. We even now."

The last thing I heard was Peanut say, "Good luck at the Throw Down, bamas . . ." I took another hit on the left side of my head and everything went even darker black than in my dream.

I can't say how much time went past before I heard Ru asking if I was okay. Then Trick. "Yo, Kid, wake up. Kid!" I had the worst headache ever. I could barely open my eyes. My right shoulder was killing me. I saw Trick's left eye wasn't but a little slit.

Ruina had some blood on his T-shirt. Big Vance was X times a factor of two just fine. You had to laugh at that. 'Cause it was mostly Vance who they wanted to pay back for the beatdown he put on Peanut. There was three thick tree branches next to the little blue tent. Now it was more a big old popped balloon than a tent.

"What happened?" I asked.

Trick told me, "They gave us a beatdown. In our sleep."

"Magno Clique?"

"No. A gang of Texas Bigfoots. Yeah, Magno Clique."

I bit my lower lip till I tasted blood. Or maybe there was already some there. "I'm so stupid. I should never been okay with them."

"Ain't a thang but a chicken wang." Trick always had a caj way of putting things to make them seem less bad. Most 'specially when things were actually real bad. Like they were just then.

Big V had to chime in. "Speak for yourself, T."

Trick didn't miss a beat. "Say what, son?"

V shook his head. "I told y'all gaylords we shoulda rolled with Lester from P.A."

I told Vance to get off the gas. "Trick was about tippin' with Lester, not you. Plus, if you never wrecked Peanut like that, Magno wouldn't of had no cause to throw a beatdown on us."

Vance got up and pointed at me. "You must be sippin' again, mane. Who paged who for help in the first place?"

That did it. I got up and shouted, "It's *your* fault, Vance! You shouldn't of wrecked Peanut bad as you did. Fat psycho!"

Vance stepped to me. I grabbed up one of the tree

branches and got ready to use it. And I do mean ready. I felt blood pump into my face and arms. Trick got between me and V and held his hand out to me. "Gimme that." Trick grabbed the stick and chucked it to the ground. He told me and Vance to shake hands. I felt real stupid about it. Like me and Vance were little kids and Trick was our Little League coach or somebody.

Then Vance moseyed over to the biggest stick that Magno had left behind. It was really more like a big ol' caveman club. He bent over and picked it up. Trick stepped to him. "What it do, V? Thought you and Kid was copacetic."

Vance was all, "Just bringing it back to B-town for Magno."

Ru was like, "You're so considerate."

"Yeah. Your moms taught me good. Real good. Know what I'm sayin'?"

"I know you cruisin' for a bruisin'." Guess Ru didn't dig Vance's gag.

We broke camp and took a path through the woods. Me and Trick out front. Big Vance and Ruina behind. Trick walked with a little limp. "They muffed my left ankle all up."

Vance was all, "We gonna muff up more than ankles."

Ru nodded. "*Cabrons* out for blood, blood's gonna flow."

The path was about to take us out of the woods. We were thirty feet from where the trail ended and a big cotton field started. You could see a red tractor and a white farmhouse way across the field on the edge of the sky.

I was like, "We in bum F-ing nowhere. How we gonna make the Throw Down?"

Trick felt around his face and shook his head. "My eye. We can't go like this."

Ruina patted me on the back. "Yo, Kid. We'll do it next year."

I got in front of the Krew and blocked them ten feet before the footpath ended. I looked at Ru. "It's funny. Last summer that's what *we* said. Right after you dogged us for Cali."

Ru shot back, "You can just keep all that jazz to yourself, Kid. I'm all paid up with the Krew now. Right or wrong?"

I rolled my shoulders up.

Trick shook his head. "No way we up for it this year, Kid. Open your peeps and look."

Vance nodded. "It's true. And it sucks donkey nads. But this ain't the year."

I shook my head and told Trick, "I'm looking. And all I see's three beat-down wussies."

Trick pushed me. Not real hard. But hard enough I knew he meant it. "You as beat down and scared as the rest of us. Wussy."

"True. But I'm still down to grind. We don't compete this year, then Magno could be the crew that makes a name for B-town. And that ain't gonna happen."

Vance was all, "Drop that concept, Kid. We gonna handle Magno Clique straight up triple O.G. thug—style. Get right up they ass before they even know it."

Ru got hyped. "Shyeah. Let's roll back to B-town, get the jump on them."

I stood my ground with Vance. "No, V. Can't you ever get it? We go head to head with Magno, but we keep it in the cypher. We're better than them. Or do you think it's the other way around?"

Vance wasn't having it. "Even saying we's down with the notion, how in the hell's we gonna get to Fifth Ward?"

Now was my chance to hustle and shine and make up for acting like a Little Leaguer earlier that morning. "Kick it right here, y'all. I'll be back."

It took me 'bout twanky minutes to sneak up close to the farmhouse and tractor. There was a bunch of wet clothes on the line. But no car in the driveway. And no one around. The tractor was a Farmall 300. A bigger model than my Paw Paw's old one. It took me a long minute to start it up. Then I had to get a feel for it. I wasn't proud of heisting a tractor from some poor cotton farmer. But how else could me and the Krew make H-town in time? Everyone in the Krew crapped cinderblocks when they saw me bounce across the field in the tractor. I tipped up to the Krew, stopped, and pointed to the five-foot rear wheels. "Check them rims. We definitely ain't sittin' on minors."

Nobody could believe I'd jacked a tractor. But the Krew jumped on and we tipped over the field to a dirt road. Big V still had the club. He opened the dash and found some Red Man chew. We all got sick off the backy 'cause we hadn't ate breakfast. I tipped away from the sun as best I could since we were still Southeast of H-town. I found a gravel road and followed it West to a blacktop road.

Before the gas even got low I pulled us over to a one-pump gas station. The guy working the station couldn'tve been older than Vance. He scoped us funny from the time he saw us. You could tell he thought we were shady. I mean for tippin' a tractor around like a slab. But he was friendly 'bout explaining the best way to get to H-town by the smaller roads. Even still, the closer we got to H-town, the worse the traffic got. Slabs kept honking and honking. Even when I tipped the Farmall on the shoulder. Two police guys rolling together in a unmarked car slowed down to stop us.

Trick leaned over. "Tell him we driving into town for repairs." But lucky for us a bling Escalade was causing major pain in the turning lane. The police guy on shotgun pointed ahead. The police guy driving took off after the Escalade. Close one. Too close. I also took the turning lane. We ditched the tractor on Lockwood Drive and Buffalo Bayou, the Southeast corner of Fifth Ward. Ru had a H-Town Throw Down flyer in his back pocket. So finding the rec center was easy peasy. I'll say it again—Ru's the smart one. I probably don't gotta tell you that our shirts weren't just dirty by then. They were downright ripe.

If you really thought about it, we were pretty lucky that the Clique had put their beatdown on us early as they did. It took more than three hours to get from them woods to the Fifth Ward. And before we hit the Throw Down we still had to get cleaned up and whatnot. Everybody pitched in the last of their change over and above entry. We found a joint called Carson's Five and Dime. The manager made Vance leave the club outside. We just barely had enough paper to buy four tall white tees. Them tall tees were cheap, plain and simple. But they were new and clean. The best place we could find to clean up was the restroom of a Krystal. I didn't even know I had a cut on my face till I checked it in the mirror.

Ru got busy slapping on Vogue yellow krump paint all graff-style to the scrapes and bruises on his face and shoulder. He held the paint stick out to me. But I'd washed my face and didn't think I was so bad off that I needed paint to cover up.

Everyone else ate hash browns and made fun of me for getting grits. Which doesn't make sense 'cause grits taste better. We walked the rest of the way to the rec center from Krystal. My shoulder, Trick's ankle, and even Ru's knee seemed better after some good eats. Plus we were washed up and changed up. Before we crossed the street to the rec center I scoped a spot called Amy's Ice Cream. "Yo, Trick. We win the prize money, we can hit that ice cream joint."

Trick nodded. "We win, we can hit a shake joint." Which wasn't really true 'cause no one but Vance was eighteen yet.

A lot of crews were just hanging outside, even though the line to get inside wasn't bad. Me and Trick walked side to side. And Vance and Ruina was behind us like regular.

You could see some of the posses giving us looks like, *We gonna destroy y'all*. But the Krew maintained its cool.

Then a line of a dozen draped-up and dripped-out slabs came swangin' and bangin' into the parking lot. Real slow-like. Most the slabs were candy color, sittin' on Vogues and Sprees. Vogues are those tires with yellow and white stripes. Sprees are those shiny rims that spin. Pretty much all the drivers were sittin' sideways, leaning up against the door and almost out the window. Everyone jammed bassed-out screwed and chopped. Nine or ten had popped trunk, a few with TV screens. And three of them glowed red neon that said 3RD WARD HUSTLERS. No one pops trunk unless they got something flashy to show off inside.

Trick was like, "Third Ward Hustlers still ballin' in the mix. Check them glass eighty-fours pokin' out." There they were. Cadillac axle extenders on the rims of the slab out front. Nothing like the baby axle extenders on my bike. They were even doper than the kind you see in a James Bond movie. You know those ones that bust out when 007 pushes the button that X, or whatever letter that guy's name is, shows him in the beginning of the movie.

One trunk glowed blue neon that said SOUTHLE & CRESTHILL'S WHAT IT DO—RIP. Another glowed purple and said POPLAR AND GREENSTONE—SUC. I think the RIP was for DJ Screw and the SUC stood for the Screwed-Up Clique.

Another slab had shiny blades, and Vance squinted and pointed. "Them blades is chopping."

Trick pointed out a red ragtop. "Scope the candy apple drop."

Ru checked out the whole lineup of slabs. "They ain't seem like b-boys."

I put down, "That's 'cause them swangas and slangas ain't. They Latrell's purple drank hookup, screwhead."

Ru looked at the third slab in the lineup. "Peep them Sprees. Why ain't we dealing?"

I told him, "'Cause we *are* b-boys."

The swangers blocked all the rest of the traffic, but didn't no one that was made to wait say a thing. The guy tippin' the slab out front looked over at the Krew. He flashed a mouthful of bling set in a platinum grill. He grinned till my eyes hurt from the sun bouncing off his grill shine.

From my side vision I scoped a real cute Thai girl. She stood behind a posse of mean-looking Thai dudes. Then I recognized who they were and pretended not to notice her. Even if I knowed she was still checking me.

Trick tapped me. "Dang. That Oriental yamp be scoping your bone zone. But them chumps be fronting like they Bangkok Dangerous."

I stayed focused ahead. "That *is* Bangkok Dangerous."

Trick looked away from the girl. "Dang! You serious?"

Ru asked, "Where they from? Shaolin, China?"

"Nah, D-town, Texas," I told him.

Big Vance asked, "Them Chinatown monkeys fittin' to throw down some kung fu?"

Trick cold corrected him. "Thai kickboxing be more like it. Why you think they named Bangkok Dangerous?"

Vance put down, "You didn't even know it was them till Kid said."

Then I recognized even more of the big crews from the b-boy magazines and Web sites. "Yo, there's Fresh Face Slim. Dang, the whole Corner Clique's in the house . . ."

Even Vance recognized a few of the crews. "Check it. The A-Town Playas."

"What?" asked Ru. "They supposed to be good?"

If he only knew. The A-Town Playas were the best ol'-skool breakers in the Southwest. Maybe even worldwide.

Me and the whole Krew turned to scope a posse of b-boys with flashy jackets that all read NAVAJO NINJAS: REPPIN AZ 500 YEARS & GOING.

Ru tried to stare down the tallest Ninja. The guy glared back and threw out a *"Nakia!"*

Ruina threw back a mean, *"Anasazi!"* right to the guy's face.

"What you tell the Ninjas?" I asked him.

Ru was all, "Basically I told them, Prep to get K-rushed.'"

I turned and scoped a bopper in that blue dress Alicia wore that one time. That throwed me. It looked hella like her. But it wasn't. Whoever it was went over and hugged the tallest Ninja. The one who talked trash to Ruina. The tallest Ninja kissed the girl. Then grinned and wiggled his tongue at Ruina. Some people gotta be bucknasty.

We kept our eyes open for Magno Clique. But couldn't none of us spot them. Once we got inside the rec center you could see posses warming up. A few unofficial one-on-one battles were even going on. There were more people there to just watch than to compete. It sort of felt like some higgledy-piggledy circus. A lot of the crowd milled all around the main floor. And a bunch of folks sat up above in two balconies. There was all kinds of people in the crowd. Yellow, brown, black, red, white, and even blue, depending how you count a Anglo dude with a face full on covered in blue tats.

Under the balcony on one side were little stands

where you could grab a Dublin Dr P. A hot dog. Fries. Candy. Or whatever. Under the balcony on the other side were a bunch of stands with graffed-up hip-hop gear. Stuff like ball caps. 'Do rags. Tees and jerseys. In the center of the hall the DJ, MC, and judges were all set up. Right next to the cypher. All around the rest of the rec center crews messed around. Some crews started warming up wherever they could grab a spot. Pretty soon all the crews from outside were inside. It got crowded in a good way. Me and the rest of the Krew practiced some basic moves in a far corner of the rec center. In the middle of a backspin I heard the MC tap his mike. But I still kept on spinning.

I was grooving through my set when I saw Vance jump up all hot and bothered. He pointed across the rec center. "Check them bung lickers." Magno Clique was way across the rec center. Cold clockin' us. You could tell the Clique was shook up. There we were. Ready to battle in fresh white tees. Big Vance had his peeps set on Peanut. He charged over in that direction, dragging the club.

I ran after him and shouted back to Trick and Ru. "Step up, y'all! Help me out here!"

I got in Vance's grill. "Stop plexin', V. Y'ain't gonna F up the Krew's shot."

Vance's stare went from Peanut to me. "Just try and

stop me, pretty boy." Vance bumped into me, still dragging the club. He walked right up to Magno Clique before me and the Krew could get there. He hoisted up the club. Everybody in the Clique backed up.

Just when me and the Krew got there, Vance chucked the club to the floor. *Bam!* Right at the Clique's feet. Vance told them, "Y'all forgot this. And you're gonna need it. Trust me."

Everybody from the Krew scoped everybody from the Clique and vice versa. Nobody in the Clique said nothing. The only thing to save us from a stare-down contest was the MC. "Yeah, yeah, yeah, *vatos*. You know what it do. But lend me your ears anyway. 'Cause I'm only gonna break it down once, feel me?"

By then Vance was chill. Him and me and the rest of the Krew walked away from the Clique. The MC's voice echoed all over the rec center. I tried to clock the MC. But he was on ground level and you couldn't see him since all around the cypher was so crowded. Even if the cypher itself was still empty. Like a hurricane eye.

The MC laid it out. "Keep it clean. Keep your tail feathers on your side of the line. One a y'all at a time. Ah-ight? Don't want the cypher to get outta hand. It's all about the love. Plus, the judges ain't having none a that in-your-face trash this year." There were four judges. All of them ol'-skool b-boys. They sat, chilling around the cypher. Debating on what crew would go against what crew. After every battle the judges whisper to the MC. He's the one and only guy at a official battle who will tell you who won. Or who lost. And which crews are in the circle next. The MC keeps it straight for the crews so everyone knows what's up. And they usually gag and joke like a mug. They're kind of like a head ref, scorekeeper, and standup comedian all rolled into one.

I practiced some windmills. I kept thinking how at the end of it all the two top crews would battle each other for first place. And I couldn't tune the MC out. "So, re-member, it ain't just about what you're doing, but about what you're *not* doing. Keep it real. But keep it pro-fessional, *mamones*. First battle. Bangkok Dangerous gonna take on the Bull Roosters. Let's do this."

The crowd went loco, including the Krew. But I kept on trying to practice my moves. Trick motioned to me. I saw the Krew head for the cypher so I followed along. We pushed our way up front, where Bangkok Dangerous was fixing to square off with the Bull Roosters.

The first guy from Bangkok Dangerous did a gainer into the cypher. He was skinny and real tall for a Oriental guy. He did a headslide over to the Bull Roosters. It was pretty tight. And a really hard move 'cause he basically jumped, then slid across the cypher on his hands and head at the same time. Then he scissor kicked around and pointed at one of the Bull Roosters with his feet. The crowd chuckled it up on that move. In b-boy competition, pointing at the other crew with your feet's a megadis. The Bangkok Dangerous crew jumped up and down and even threw their hood up, which is sort of like putting up a gang sign. You hardly ever see it in a real competition with judges there and all. The Bull Roosters worked hard pretending like the moves weren't nothing but a thang.

The first Bull Rooster into the cypher warmed up with some kung fu–style uprock. Then he busted a backflip. He went into a vertical pushup, where you push up off the floor with your feet pointing to the ceiling. The same cat broke into an insane corkscrew. That's where you spin clockwise on your head. Freeze. Then spin counterclockwise. He kept doing it and doing it till his whole crew and even the whole crowd went loco.

Ruina was like, "Dang."

Then Vance. "Double dang."

The Bull Roosters jumped up and down. Then, as a gag, all the Bull Roosters cock-a-doodle-doed like roosters and raised up their hands on their heads like rooster crests. Goofing like that can be half the fun. Like how footballers sometimes act a fool in the end zone after a big TD. I saw Trick and Vance give a look like, *Aww, hell.* Or maybe that's just what I was thinking. It looked like Magno wasn't the only crew we had to stress about if we wanted to go the distance and make B-town shine under the Krush Krew tag. But we knowed that from the get-go.

BREAKBEAT 12
STEP YOUR GAME UP

Seeing the Bull Roosters' mad skills just made me want to practice harder. I went back to the corner and busted out some uprock. An old guy like Mr. Kaprinski's age, maybe thirty-whatever years old, stood in a little booth. He wore real dark sunglasses. That didn't seem right. 'Specially 'cause it was inside and none too bright. The stand he ran sold a bunch of graffed-up gear. Even though I couldn't see through the sunglasses I could tell he was scoping me. He wiped his nose like he had a cold or whatever. Some dude rolled up to the booth and asked sunglasses guy 'bout a jersey that said BIG PIMPIN on it. Sunglasses Guy waved the dude off, and you could tell the dude was pissed. He wiped his nose again and looked back over my way. It sort of bothered me. But I just ignored him like he wasn't even there.

I went from a vertical handspin to a backspin to a freeze. All the moving around got me loosened up and feeling good. When I stood up the guy was still peeping me through them shades. I busted out a combo that ended with me pointing both my feet at the guy. He took the sunglasses off and nibbled on the end of them. It gave me a bad feeling in my gut. Like maybe the guy was some kind of pervert molester or whatever.

I heard the MC laying things out real fast. "Yeah, yeah. That was some bombastic dopeness. Winner between Bull Roosters and Bangkok Dangerous. Judge one give it to Bangkok Dangerous. Judge two call it a draw. What kind of judging's that? Judge three hand it to Bull Roosters. And judge four . . . Bull Roosters." The MC kept breaking it down. "Next up, we got the Valley Boyz versus . . . Krush Krew? I ain't ever heard of these homeboys, but they sound eighties." MCs are pretty much allowed to mess with all the crews now and again. But they don't do it in a mean way. More like how them Oscar MCs mess with them big-shot movie stars at their award thing.

The crowd chuckled it up, but I didn't pay that any mind. I was just stressing that we were on deck next. Me and the Krew hadn't knowed we were gonna be that early in the lineup. I made for the cypher. I pushed my way through some folks and saw the Krew scoping around for me. Some guy elbowed me on my right side. I turned and he told me sorry. I could tell it was a accident so I didn't make nothing of it. Then I saw Sunglasses Guy pushing his way to the cypher from my right. I figured there wasn't a law against that. Even if he did look like some kind of pervert molester, like I said.

The comp was already lined up on their side of the cypher. They had one b-girl in their crew, even if they were named the Valley Boyz. She was way taller than anybody from the Krew and had slim muscles and looked mean as a bobcat. I joined up with the Krew on the other side. Each crew has one half the circle. But when you're on deck you can throw down on the other crew's side as much as you want. Really get up in their grill. The MC grinned. "Ah-ight, DJ, hit it." And the DJ dropped a funky beat.

Trick shook his head. "Mane, I can DJ better than that." Maybe. But all I could think about was hitting the cypher.

Some little guy with Jheri curls was the first of the Valley Boyz to hit the cypher. He had a few Fred Astaire—type moves. He was good and he got right up in Ruina's grill. Ru just played it off like *de nada*. He had some Fred Astaire moves of his own. When it was his turn to mash in the cypher he showed up the Jheri curls kid but good. Ru really shined with a krump Charlie Chaplin tiptoe walk with chest pops and torso jerks and all. You could tell the crowd liked it, but Jheri curls and the rest of the Valley Boyz played like they weren't even checking Ru's L.A. stylins.

The swollest guy from the Valley Boyz hit the cypher and threw down some wicked uprock in Vance's direction. Then he busted out a gang of Boston crabs. They're basically turtles, but your legs are more spread and your body more up in the air. Vance hit the ground with two circles of six-step then did a icy-ice. It didn't look too good since it's even easier than a turtle, let alone a Boston crab. But Vance made up for it by doing a mess of bellymills. Vance was swoll, but he could still get his feet circling way up and around him on his bellymills. He closed with a nut-grab freeze. Me and the Krew high-fived on our side of the cypher.

The skinniest Valley Boyz dude got up in Trick's grill with some wannabe locking and popping. And he didn't even hit the floor once. Trick struck back with some realness. I mean, Trick wasn't even a poplocker, but he could bite anything whoever else threw down. And make it look even better. Trick did a Colt 45. Then hit the deck. He threw down a gang of eggbeaters, those windmills where your hands are way high up on your hips. He spun like a top, shoulder to shoulder, his feet making circles way up in the air. He didn't even bother with T-flares. He'd already full on destroyed the comp. T-flares would have just been rubbing the Valley Boyz' snouts in it.

The tall mean-looking b-girl got in my face. But it wasn't like she had real style. Her best move was a lame wannabe 1990. That's where you do a one-hand handstand and use your second hand to spin around on the first. Before she was even out of the cypher I was throwing down a full-scale attack. I sort of felt bad, 'cause she was a bopper and all. But her face looked so mean that I didn't feel bad for long. I broke out from six-step to a headspin. Then froze my feet so they were pointing at her. Megadis.

The Krew jumped up and down behind me. That got me hyped. I pushed up vertical. Then windmilled. But on the first rotation I hit my shoulder hard. So hard I wanted to scream out loud. But I didn't. The pain was bad enough I wanted to crawl out of the cypher. And keep crawling into a hole someplace and hide. I scoped the Krew. I saw how beat down Trick and Ru looked. They'd gave 200 percent. I had to keep on keeping on.

I spun on one hand, 1990-style. Then landed solid on my feet. Mane. It was on and so was I. I closed it out with some airplanes, windmills where your arms extend out to each side. After my final rotation I nailed a nut-grab suicide. Dang. My shoulder hurt a lot and my back hurt a little. But that finish got the crowd way 'gized. Sunglasses Dude still clocked me. But I didn't even stress. I stood up. My right shoulder made clicking and cracking noises when it moved. But it wasn't so bad that I couldn't just take my mind off it.

Me and the whole Krew couldn't believe how good we did. All we could do was wait to hear who the judges would give it to. I felt sweat drip down my face. I rubbed it off and saw it was blood from the cut over my eye.

The MC got on the mike. "All in all, the judges give it to . . . Krump Krew. I mean *Krush* Krew. Ha ha, that paint done throwed me." The crowd went loco with us. There was a few small boos here and there. Must have been some peeps up from the Valley in the pack. Everyone in the Krew gave everyone else a hug.

But too much hugging with your boys always makes you feel a little fruity. So we broke up doing all that pretty quick. Trick and Vance ran off to the bathroom. I needed to drink down some water and chill for a bit. At the fountain I heard someone talk behind me with a New Yorker-type voice.

"Kudos. A little token for you."

I turned. Sunglasses Guy. He held out a ball cap with a cool design on it. I asked him why he was giving it to me. He was all, "Get 'em from Shenzhen for peanuts."

I'd never met anybody named Shenzhen and couldn't tell you who he was talking about.

It was a dope-looking ball cap. At first I wasn't sure if I should take it or not. But I couldn't see no harm. I told him, "Thanks."

He nodded. "Excellent work out there." He scoped the cut on my face. "Ouch. How'd that happen? And tell me, how old are you?"

"Eighteen. Nex week." That was kind of a lie since it was really more like a few months. With old people it's usually best to front like you're older if you want to max the respect you get.

He nodded. "Good. Nothing but legal headaches with minors."

I figured he was talking 'bout me doing some pervert-type stuff for paper. He was lucky I didn't hit him then and there on his nose. I told him, "I don't do nothing like that."

"Like . . . ? Oh, you thought I wanted to . . . No. That's not what I'm getting at."

I kept moving for the water fountain. "I gotta get some water."

I leaned over the faucet and Sunglasses Guy was all, "Wait."

I turned and saw him reach into his case. "I wouldn't trust the tap." He pulled out a half-full bottle of water.

I went ahead and drank from the faucet even if it was H-town H_2O. I stood up. "Tastes ah-ight. Why you wear them sunglasses inside?" I figured I'd call him out on his pervert molester ways.

"Sensitive eyes. And they're damn good at spotting talent."

Maybe he wasn't a pervert molester. But I decided he wasn't 100 percent legit as a scout. I told him, "I gotta get back to the Krew."

I walked off. And made sure he wasn't following after me. I used my left hand to rub the sting out of my right shoulder. But I couldn't get it to feeling 100 again. I tried on the green ball cap and it fit like a glove. 'Cept for on my head and not my hand.

BREAKBEAT 13
THE PEOPLE'S CHAMP

After a gang of battles between other crews, the MC called us up again. "Next up it's Magno Clique going head to head with Krush Krew. Gotta say, both crews is up-and-comers, y'all." I didn't know it was gonna go down till I heard it over the PA. I was amped. But my gut felt tense.

Sunglasses Guy got right up on the edge of the cypher to watch us battle the Clique. At first no one in Magno could even look us straight in the eye. So what about the beatdown we took? There we were. Ready to mash. Straight up grinders, mane.

The MC was all, "Ah-ight, *maladitos*. This is it. Down to the semifinal, man-ees. Magno Clique, get on deck."

The DJ dropped a beat and Izzle moved into the cypher with some uprock. But he didn't step to Ru. He hit the ground and did three circles of six-step. Then he went into helicopters, jumping over his right leg again and again with his left. He transitioned to genies, them windmills where you cross your arms over your chest. Still spinning around and around shoulder to shoulder, he moved his hands to the small of his back and did a gang of handcuffs. A dang good set, but he wobbled on his outro freeze.

I leaned over to Trick and was like, "Yo, T, my right shoulder's burning like a mug."

He was all, "How bad is it?"

"I don't know. Can you hear it?" I rotated my shoulder close to his ear.

He nodded his head when he heard it clicking and popping. "No pressure, but this is our chance to take Magno down public-style in the cypher, mane."

"No shit, T. We'd be in B-town right now pickin' our snouts if I didn't rally y'all in the a.m."

T nodded. "Dang. My bad."

I just tried to keep my focus off my shoulder and on what was happening in the cypher. Ru jumped in with a gainer. He put down a krump walk complete with mouth chatters. He looked like one of them talking dummies that sit on a real guy's lap. Ru chucked in a few applejacks that a Russian soldier couldn't of kicked out any better. He finished with perfect nutcrackers. The whole crowd laughed and Izzle just shook his head.

Steamed as a mug, Peanut locked on Vance. He stepped into the cypher with some tight boomerangs. His legs in a V, circling around and around with only his hands touching ground. Then he busted out with rubber-bands, popping up from his back, falling back, kipping up, falling back, again and again. On his last kip-up he transitioned to a turtle, spinning with his face to the ground. Around and around. He picked up speed and comboed to crickets. Springing up and down on both his hands and still spinning circle after circle. To finish, he switched up to jackhammers, bouncing up and down on just his left hand, still spinning fast as a mug.

After Peanut's tight set, Vance had his work cut out. Cool as a cube, he stepped right up with some icy-ices. Then did a handglide. Next he busted into some Boston crabs, spinning face-down, around and around, his legs spread wide and his upper body high in the air. He transitioned to a backspin, came to a stop, and kipped up. Soon as he popped up from his back and landed on his feet, he dropped into his perfection. Bellymills. His swoll legs circled around and around over him. They almost hit

Peanut. Twice. But never did. The judges, and the whole crowd, was on edge.

Dap put on a ugly face for Trick and broke into the cypher with a Colt 45 J.B.'d of been jealous of. He dropped, face to the ground, legs scissor kicking back and forth, almost hitting Trick. He transitioned to flares, and would have got a gold medal if it was the Olympics. Next, Dap did a 2000, spinning around in a two-handed handstand. He switched up to a 2001, staying in a handstand but spinning on the back of just one hand. You gotta admit the boy had skills. He outroed his set with a mess of halos, a cross between headspins and windmills. Dap went back to his half of the cypher.

I knew Trick was stressed that his ankle was still a little muffed up from the beatdown. But he stepped onto the floor with authority. After some uprock footwork, he headslid all the way across the cypher. His feet almost smacked Dap in his grill. It was on for realio. Next Trick broke out a gang of eggbeaters. Rolling from shoulder to shoulder, hands on his hips, his legs making big circles in the air. He did three flares that might not have took Olympic gold after Dap's set. But would of for sure got silver. Keeping his legs tight together, Trick changed his flares up to T-flares.

Trick ended his set with a perfect freeze, pointing both his feet at Dap. Mane, them T-flares, plus the freeze, might just have snatched the gold right from under Dap's snout. Soon as T stepped out of the cypher he got behind me. He sat on his booty and stretched out his busted ankle. He was real smart about it and stayed hid away from the judges. Not like they should care, since he was out of the cypher. But you never want to seem weak in a battle. Even outside the ring.

Warren stumbled into the cypher all caj, like it wasn't nothing but a thang. But I could tell he was stressin' underneath it all. He got in my face with some uprock. Then he hit the deck. A vertical pushup got switched up to airswipes. Warren rotated around and around, staying horizontal to the ground. He fell to his back, kipped up, and airwalked all over the deal. His flow was dang tight and got me stressed. 'Specially 'cause I scoped the judges look at each other and nod their heads about it.

Warren got right up in my grill again with his airwalk. He poplocked my new green ball cap right off my head with a flick of the hand. No touching allowed in competition, so I looked over at the judges. They just shook their heads and busted up laughing. Mane, was I steamed. Ready to blow. But that's just what Warren wanted. So I lowered my pressure gauge from 100 to 90. From 90 to 80. And all the way down to 0, ten degrees at a time. Warren fell back to the ground and threw my ball cap through his legs right back at me. He ended with a nut grab that had everyone but the Krew busting up laughing. Nut grabs do a couple things at once: dis the comp and get your own crew, and usually most the crowd, chuckling.

Right then I saw Vance rush past me and get into it with Warren. Pretty soon the whole Clique was jumping on V and it looked like all hell was gonna break loose. The MC was all, "Break it up, crews, break it up!" Me and Trick yanked V back with everything we had and got him off Warren right quick. Most the crowd around the cypher backed up, scared. The MC shook his head, all, "Points off for both crews." I scoped the judges. From all their chuckling I could tell the scuffle wasn't big enough for them to stop the battle. So long as no one's been hurt and the physicality's kept on the mind-messing tip, b-boy judges are pretty chill. Even when you technically done broke the rules.

I put my cap back on and hit the cypher with a forward flip. My uprock was on point and loosened me up before I hit the deck for a vertical pushup. From there I switched up to windmills. But after one rotation I hit my right shoulder again. Real hard. All I wanted was for the Krew to take Magno down on the floor. And be the first b-boy crew to really put B-town on the radar. Trick saw me stretch my right shoulder and knew that it was hurting worse. "Step your game up, partner." But what he didn't know 'bout was my secret perfection. That is, supposing I could do it.

I knew the judges would take points off if I held my set up. So quick as a wink I dropped to a headstand, then got my left arm spinning me around and around in a headspin. The whole room was a blur of color and motion. I amped up my everyday headspin to a drill headspin. I twisted my legs together and pushed them to the ceiling, spinning faster and faster on top of my head. Then I pushed up into a spinning handstand. The deep beat of the music was the only thing from outside that came in true and clear. Even though everything was a blur, I felt power from the crowd come into the cypher. I was 'gized like a mug. There was no pain in my shoulder. Or anywhere. Time to go for my perfection.

Using both hands, I popped up onto my feet. I ran at the Clique and nailed the one and a half forward flip. I felt a little dizzy, but I transitioned to airflares no prob. That got the crowd going nuts. If those Olympic judges could of seen me maybe the gold would of even been mine. My suicide was the best I'd ever done off a flare. Even though I slammed to the ground pretty much flat on my back, I still jammed my muffed-up shoulder pretty bad.

The ceiling spun and spun. I heard Trick. He sounded far off. "You did it, Kid!"

Then Ru. "Mane!"

And Vance. "Shyeah!"

Still on the ground, I looked up and smiled. The Krew, and pretty much the whole crowd, went ape-loco.

The MC was all, "*Ni madres*, if I was a judge I wouldn't wanna be a judge right now. It's a tough call, *carbons*."

Trick helped me up off the ground. I whispered to him, "I done killed my shoulder on the suicide."

Trick smiled. "Yeah, *and* you done killed Magno."

Me and the rest of the Krew waited for the word from the judges. I was still breathing hard. It felt like a long hour before the MC got all the votes figured. The MC shook his head and scoped us. "Hard to believe, but these youngsters take it unanimous. Krush Krew all the way."

We jumped up and down so high we near hit the ceiling. A whole mess of folks from other crews, and peeps who were just there to watch, came running over and slapped us on the back. There was even a gang of boppers who hoofed it over and tried to touch us. Like, just to see if we were real.

I scoped the Clique and they all looked beat down. Bad. I mean peed-on-with-no-soap bad. Like way worse than the Krew had looked early in the morning after the animal beatdown they'd put on us. It made me figure getting your body hurt's not near so bad as having props and love and respect snatched away from you. When it comes to the cypher, one crew's loss is another crew's gain. And vice versa. That's just the way it is. And always was. And always will be. There's only so much honor to go around.

Me and the rest of the Krew got mad love from the whole rec center. Then everybody in the balconies shouted, "Krush Krew, Krush Krew, Krush Krew . . ." Pretty soon everybody in the whole deal was in on it. "Krush Krew, Krush Krew, Krush Krew . . ." Over and over. Again and again. Vance picked me up like I was a kid and chucked me up onto his shoulders. He lugged me through the mix of folks for a long second. Like I was the people's champ or somebody. But really it was the whole Krew, grinding together, that was the champ.

In the background I heard the MC. "Settle down, settle down. After a little breather, we gonna get the final showdown. Bull Roosters versus Krush Krew. Fifteen minutes, y'all. Then back to the cypher."

Magno Clique didn't even have it in them to come over and give us props. They headed for the exit, and right quick too. Vance put me down, then jumped up and down and shouted after them, "We ain't even got started on y'all bops. Y'all can roll, but ya can't hide. Feel me?"

Everybody in the Krew gave a quick hug and Ru was like, "We did it! We beat Magno Clique! Where'd that move come from, Kid?"

I just rolled my shoulders up and played like it wasn't nothing but a thing. But then I hugged Trick. "We put B-town on the map!"

The MC walked over and wiped sweat off his face. He grinned at me. "Stop flossin'. Y'all ain't got the game sewed up just yet. That was the semifinal. Y'all still got the final. Know what I'm sayin'?"

I couldn't stop grinning from ear to ear. So what if we were flossin' a bit? We beat Magno and put B-town on the b-boy map. I looked at the MC. "Not really. Way I see it, we already done won the final." The MC nodded like he sort of got it. I was desert thirsty from the battle and told the MC, "I'm more thirsty than a triple-hump camel."

He patted me on the back. "Then go get you some *agua*. Y'all *moquitos* doing great. Keep it coming."

Me and Trick headed for the fountains. Two young boppers wearing lots of makeup followed after me and Trick. But mostly after Trick I think. At least I didn't want to think about them clockin' me like that since Alicia was already my girl and stuff.

Trick leaned over to me. "See that. Now that we beat Magno Clique in the semis, them bops wanna get with us, mane."

I was all, "Nah, they just clockin' us. I still can't believe we did it!"

Trick shook his head and kept it quiet enough so the ladies couldn't hear. "With them kindsa dames, no such thing as just clockin'. Poonani's poonani, Kid. And I ain't had none in a while. You?"

Trick didn't know I was still a, well, you know. I still hadn't been with a girl in that way just yet.

"Nah. Not much lately."

"What about Leesha? Y'all been chillin' a lot. You damn well been slidin' on that bopper. Right?"

"Daily. I mean, nah. I don't know . . ." I didn't really want to talk about it, so I made off for the fountain by myself. I heard Trick call after me and I pretended not to hear. The water was cold and felt good going down my throat and into my belly. It tasted even better when I thought on how we'd beat Magno Clique.

When I stood up Sunglasses Guy scoped me again. He walked over with a big grin. I was set to thump him. I told him, "Look, I gotta focus before the nex battle."

He nodded. "After the final battle, I'd like to buy you dinner and talk business."

My gut tensed and my chest bowed up. My right hand tightened to a fist. "I told you. I don't do that stuff."

"Look, let me explain, Kid B. It's Kid B, right?" I nodded. "Kid. You know what a talent scout does. Yes?"

"Yeah. They scout talent."

"That's right. And that's what I do. I scout talent. And I think I found some here today."

"So, what does that mean?"

He took off the sunglasses. His eyes were all red and stuff. "That's what I'd like to talk with you about at dinner."

If he was legit, I figured he would tell me who he worked with. I told him straight up, "I gotta get back to the cypher."

Heading back, I heard him call after me. "I'm Barry Weiss. Do you know who I know? You ever been to New York? You ever heard of G-La?"

Mane. I didn't turn back right away. But I almost slammed into one of the poles that held the rec center roof up. Maybe he was lying. But what if it was true? When I did turn back I saw he wasn't scoping me no more. He pulled out a bling cell phone. I started to walk back to him but stopped behind the pole and perked my ears up.

I didn't want him to know I was listening in. So I kind of stayed hid. It was hard to catch everything he said. "Dettori? . . . When's he getting back? . . . No, forget it, take a message then. Barry Weiss . . . *Weiss*—do I *sound* like Barry White? Yeah. Tell him the backup dancer problem's solved . . . No, no, no . . . this kid's better than that. And he's whiter than snow . . . I'm telling you, he's half Elvis, half Eminem, and half Paul Wall . . . Yeah, I damn well know that totals up to one and a half. And that's what I'm saying . . ."

I could get paid to get down with G-La . . . Dang. That would be hella better than grinding at the oil refinery with Earl. So what if Vance's dad was foreman there and might have my back?

BREAKBEAT 14
'BOUT THAT GREEN

Going up against the Bull Roosters in the final was more about having fun than stressing about the win. Trick was first on deck. Colt 45, scissor kicks, T-flares, eggbeaters. Pretty much the whole nine. With a tight freeze to wrap it. The first Bull Rooster stepped the game up by doing everything Trick did one notch better. Plus he added a double 99—basically a 2000 handstand where you spin on the back of one hand. Then the back of the other hand. Back and forth time and again. A sick move that none of the Krew could top.

Vance put down his best set yet. He wrapped it by nailing a fly gang of bellymills like nobody's business. But I can't lie. The next Bull Rooster had a dope set and took him out. He closed with a mess of supertight tombstones, windmills where his legs were closed and his body was in a L shape. And he didn't touch the deck with his hands even once.

Ru came in strong with a gainer and shook out some krump. Then he sprang back and forth with a bunch of real strong broncos. He threw down handcuffs like a mug, his legs doing circles over him, hands tucked behind his back. He switched his hands to the front and grabbed his Vienna sausage without stopping the windmill motion. The next Bull Rooster was pretty sick. He had red and white krump battle paint on his face. He macked Ru by shaking out some Compton-level krump. Then a bunch of coindrops. Coindrops are flares where you drop onto your back and bounce back into flares and keep going. I didn't even know what they were till Trick told me.

I was on deck and drilled a headspin but lost momentum. I felt the muscles in my right shoulder spazz and lock up. I tried airtwists and flares. But all my muscles everywhere burned. Nothing worked right anymore. I face-planted. The whole crowd breathed in about it. I knew the finals were on my shoulders. 'Specially the muffed-up right one. And that lawyer Murphy, or whoever made up that go-wrong law, must have been there in the rec center, 'cause my right shoulder did get out of whack again. I tried another airflare. When I fell the second time, I knew I was finished.

When I thought on it for a quick second and it didn't weigh too heavy. The Krew had already beat Magno Clique. The Bull Roosters would have just been icing. That's never near as important as the cake. Just as a gag I closed with a one-armed worm and got the whole crowd, the Krew, the judges, and even all the Bull Roosters, laughing. The Bull Rooster after me finished out his set with a triple halo to a suicide. That was almost unsportsmanlike since they already had us beat so bad.

The MC went and chatted with the judges. He didn't take too long. He grabbed up the mike. "Yo, it's final, and it's unanimous. The judges all give it up to the Bull Roosters." The crowd agreed with the judges. I did too. The Bull Roosters acted like regular comedians. They ran around again in a circle, with their hands on top their heads like rooster crests. Then everyone in the Krew high-fived everyone in the Bull Roosters. Like how it's supposed to be with true b-boys.

I found a empty bench where no one was and sat down. My head was down but I scoped Barry coming. He didn't run right over. He stood away and let me stay solo for a long second. Then he came over and stood by me. "That was a good effort. But you coulda drank more water and maybe paced yourself better."

I didn't say anything. And even when he asked me, "Mind if I sit?" I still didn't say anything. He sat down. "All you guys did good out there."

"Yeah. 'Cept I muffed up my shoulder."

"I'm sorry to hear that. You should have it looked at."

"Looked at?"

"Yes. By a doctor." He stood up. "Look, I'm starving. Dinner's your call. You up for sushi?"

I shook my head. "Nah. My stomach can't deal with Chinese." Then I had a idea. "But I saw a ice cream spot across the way."

"Ice cream for dinner?"

"You said my call."

Barry nodded. I stood up. "What about the Krew?"

"Invite them. And ice cream's on me. But I want to have a meeting just you and me. Okay?"

I went over and got the whole Krew together and asked them, "Y'all ready for some free ice cream?"

Everybody was confused and Vance was like, "We got thangs to tend to in Beaumont."

"Free ice cream," I told them.

Trick shook his head. "I still wanna get with them honeys."

"Bring 'em."

Trick asked me, "Yeah, and how we gonna pay? We just barely got the paper to make B-town."

I pointed. "That dude." Barry stood like thirty or forty feet away.

"Who the hell's that?" Trick asked.

"Talent scout. From New York. He work with G-La." When I told them I saw they were impressed.

Barry followed me and the Krew outside. The two boppers jonesing for Trick tagged along too. There was a major crowd chilling out front. And I saw the girl in the blue dress from before we went into the rec center. The one who looked like Leesha. She caught me scoping her but she wasn't miffed about it. She sort of flipped her hair over her shoulder and gave me a little smile. It was nice. Not as nice as that little Alicia smile. But still nice. I thought about maybe going over and saying hi. But I knew I wouldn't. And for a second I even thought I smelled that pretty Leesha smell. But the girl in the blue dress was like fifty feet off, and I never was a bloodhound. That Alicia smell got even stronger, and someone tapped my left shoulder. "You deserve better, *bebé*." It was Alicia! Dang! I was so psyched to see her standing there I near did a flare suicide on the spot. Leesha must have knowed I was only scoping that girl in the blue 'cause she reminded me of her.

I smiled and told her, "I *got* better, *bebé*." Then real slow-like I pulled her to me. Me and her kissed right then and there in the middle of the whole crowd. Like no one was even around us at all. I can't tell you how long we kissed. But we weren't in a rush and it felt like a good long time. So what if the Krew and Barry had to wait a little spell?

Teresa had her moms's Caprice Classic station wagon parked in the rec center lot. And I came to find out she'd been the one to drive Alicia to H-town. Everybody started for the ice cream spot, and Alicia touched one of the marks on my face from the Magno beatdown. She shook her head. "You and the Krew were off the chain."

"You saw everything? Even the battle with Magno? You saw my perfection?"

She smiled up at me and nodded. Teresa was way more quiet than her usual talk-on self. And I felt a little bad about how I never showed her any love. I patted her on the shoulder. "Yo, Resa. Thanks for bringing Alicia and being here and all."

Teresa was like, "Y'all were pretty good."

"Sorry for, you know . . ."

"Me and you's cool, Kid. But let's not overdo it."

I nodded since I knew what she meant.

Inside the ice cream spot me and Barry sat in a booth on one side of the place. I guess Barry wanted me and him to be by ourselves. The Krew, and Trick's new dames, was way over on the other side of the place.

And Alicia and Teresa had a little round table right next to the Krew.

The furniture was done up with a lot of cool colors, and the whole spot had lots of fancy decorations and stuff you mostly didn't see in Beaumont. Barry wasn't paying much attention to the waitress. She had a shiny little gold metal thing glued on her forehead. Barry opened up a napkin and put it on his lap. "I'm a chocolate fiend. What flavor floats your boat, Kid?"

"Vanilla, I guess."

"Where's the adventure in that?" He told the waitress, "Bring him one of everything."

She was like, "One sample of everything?"

"No. One *scoop* of everything you got."

"Sir, we have a total of twenty flavors."

I was all, "Twanky flavors? Dang!"

Barry nodded to the waitress. "I guess that adds up to twenty scoops. Oh, and two scoops of chocolate for me. And can you put some chocolate syrup on it. And some of those chocolate sprinkle things. I don't know what they're called."

"Chocolate sprinkles?" she asked. I thought it was funny, but Barry was focusing real hard on what he wanted.

"Right. And do you have fudge chunks?"

"Yes, sir."

"And throw a few crumbled Oreos on it. But I don't want that white stuff from the middle of the cookie." He turned over my direction and patted his belly. "Goes right to my gut."

I looked over to check on the Krew and Alicia. She smiled at me and gave me one of those girl-type waves, just using the fingers. Anyway, pretty soon the waitress had the whole table at me and Barry's booth filled with scoops. It looked like a lot more than twanky. I could never eat all the scoops. The smartest thing was to try a little bit from each one, then decide which ones I liked best and finish those. But by the time I got around once, I forgot which ones were best. So I just ate on the vanilla scoop like I asked for to begin with.

The waitress brought out the last two scoops and put them on the table next to us. Barry asked her, "You think of yourself as a crow or a swan?"

She got throwed. "I'm not . . . I don't know what you mean." She touched that shiny thing glued on her forehead. "Is it my *bindi*?"

Barry talked to her all funny. "If you ever get the opportunity to do an ashram, well, I can't recommend it highly enough. I studied the Mahabharata under Baba Ramesh, and the man's a genius."

The waitress asked, "Who?"

"Baba Ramesh. The guru. He . . . never mind. So, you've got this crow, right? And, basically, he meets a swan and starts to hang out with him, you follow?" She nodded and Barry just kept on with his story. "So, the crow hangs out with the swan so much he starts thinking he's a swan too, right? And one day he takes a drink from a pond and he sees his reflection and he can't get over it. That he doesn't look like a swan."

Barry grinned up at her and put a big spoonful of fudge and chocolate into his mouth, which about made me want to puke. He talked to her with his mouth full. "So, the crow rubs himself on this white-powder rock till he turns white, and then, well, it's been a long time . . . Then, never mind that, okay? My question is this, this I ask you." He held up his hand for a second. "Don't give me your answer. Are you a crow or a swan?"

"Could I . . ."

Barry held his hand up to interrupt her.

"Don't answer me. It's a question for you."

The waitress got throwed again. But she nodded before she walked away. I guess the whole thing was sort of how Barry got his mack on. When I was in the middle of the vanilla scoop, Barry asked, "How well you know New York?"

"I know it's a big city." It sounded kind of dumb right after it left my mouth. Too late to swallow it back down.

"Yeah, New York's a big city. And that's exactly why you're gonna love it, Kid."

Just then I saw that Ru was standing by me and Barry's table. Ru scoped Barry and asked him, "What's to say you ain't gonna use Kid once and put him on the first Greyhound back to B-town?"

Barry scoped Ru. "Excuse me? This isn't your conversation."

Ru came back with, "Maybe I'm making it my conversation, shiesty mo."

I tried to stand up. But it was hard to in the booth. "Ru."

Before I could get out the booth, Barry was handing it

to Ru. "An anti-Semite. Nice. You're the trick biker Kid told me about. Let me guess. You signed a contract with a thousand-dollar advance?" Barry kept his eyes on Ru. Like he was reading him. "No. It was a three-G advance. Wow. A bigtimer. You burned through it in less than ten days. Spent it all on crap tequila, skunkweed, and second-rate head from nasty L.A. skanks."

Ru looked at the ground. But Barry kept on. "Inside four months you owed some two-bit shark a G or three. Right? You stopped showing up on time to your gigs. Drank, smoked, and jacked off whatever little talent you mighta had. Got cut off and shipped back to the dirty South. That about cover it?"

Ru didn't have anything to come back with.

Barry was like, "Go back and finish your ice cream." Barry nodded over to me. "We got real deals and real plans to make."

Ru dragged ass back to the Krew's table. Even if my business wasn't his business, I still felt bad for him. But it was like Barry seemed more real after that. Like he wasn't just fronting 'bout being a scout and all.

Barry scoped me. "So. Like I was saying, Kid. New York's got something for everybody. How'd you like to get on a plane to New York next week?"

"I don't know, Barry. There's the Krew. You know,

and my girl and family and stuff. In B-town. Plus, I'm scared of planes."

Barry leaned in and talked in a low voice. "It's about you, Kid. Not about your partner, your family, your dog, any of that baggage, or what have you."

"We ain't got a dog."

Barry grinned like he thought I told a gag or something. "That was a good one, Kid. You'll sign a basic ninety-day management contract, with a renewal option that I can choose to exercise, or not. Trust me. Ninety days go by in a snap." He even snapped his fingers when he said it.

"Ninety days?" That sounded like a real long minute, not a snap. I mean, that was basically like a whole summer from beginning to end.

"With a renewal option. Have your family lawyer check it out."

"Yeah, right. Hey, Barry. What about the Krew?"

"What about them?"

"Can't they come too?"

Barry shook his head. "Sorry, Charlie, I only need you." He looked at my face and pointed to his cheek. I used my sleeve to wipe some ice cream off the left side of my mouth.

"In any case, we won't have you sign the contract for another week. After you turn eighteen. That way we can avoid all the parental consent B.S."

Then Barry got all in a rush and yelled over to the waitress. He snapped his fingers. "Ayy, I got a plane to catch."

I told him, "I never been on a airplane."

"That'll change in a couple days."

"I'm scared about planes. I mean, I never taken one. But, you know."

"Everything's a little scary the first time around. Even getting laid, right? Did you know flying's a factor of twenty-five times safer than driving?"

"That's twenty-five hundred percent."

Barry squinted to do the math. "You're right. Now look . . ." He reached into his jacket pocket and pulled out five one-hundred-dollar bills. "All good relationships are based on trust, yes? And I trust you, Kid. As a good faith gesture on my part, I'm advancing you five hundred dollars. That will come out of your pocket once you're in New York. You understand?" I nodded. I felt my eyes swell up a little when I scoped all that paper. He handed it to me. I tried to act regular fumbling it into my pocket.

Barry paid the bill with a all-gold credit card. I seen a twanky-dollar bill just sitting on the table. "Yo, Barry. You left that."

"Yeah. Didn't tip her on my card."

I nodded my head like I got what he was saying.

"I'll book you a Monday flight to New York."

"Yo, Barry. I was thinking 'bout maybe if I could take a train instead."

Barry's face showed he didn't get it. "It's a pretty long haul to New York."

ALICIA VERSUS MY WORD

I broke my first hundred ever. Tipping back to Beaumont that night with Teresa, Leesha, and the Krew felt funny. Like everything was happening to someone else. That someone else would get to go to New York. How could a green scrapper like me be so lucky all at once like that? I woke up early that Sunday morning and told Earl about everything. I crept into Dad's room and told him too. But he was so far gone on the bottle he only caught half of what I was throwing out. I went to my bedroom and got to packing up my stuff. I didn't have all the posters down off the wall just yet and Dad came in. He looked at the posters that were still up like it was the first time he seen them. And maybe it was the first time he ever really looked at them.

"Breakdancing for G-La? What the hell sort of vocation is that?"

I told him, "They already paying me."

I pulled out three of the hundred-dollar bills. I'd already used part of one bill to help Teresa out on gas paper. Plus for some dealings I had with King Tut. And just in case Dad was gonna take all the paper he saw I wanted to keep a hundred-dollar bill for me. I kept it in that secret little pocket everyone's got in their jeans—you know the one. Lori walked into the room without a knock or anything.

Dad just kept on. "B-boying . . . What the hell kind of crap is it? What's it mean anyway? It's for delinquents, right? What about high school? Don't hand me a story, Kid."

"I don't need high school. I'm gonna do the GRE thing. And I can show you what b-boying is," I told him. "I'm gonna show you . . ."

Dad crossed his arms and looked mean. "Okay, Kid. Show me."

"I can't right now."

"Why not?"

"Make her leave."

"She's my *wife*, so get used to it."

"Yeah, well, she'll never be my *moms*. So get used to *that*."

Real cold she said, "Your real mama's dead, Breslin. Get over it."

Dad's voice choked and he told Lori to get out the room. She did. He smacked me upside the head. Then grabbed me by the neck and pulled me to the mirror that was hung up above my dresser. He yelled, "Look!"

I scoped my face in the mirror. "What?"

"At your face. Look at your face. What do you see?"

"Huh? Nothing."

He cuffed me square upside my head. Hard enough that it dropped me right to the deck. I just held my head. He yelled, "Get it through that thick bull head of yours, Kid. You're *white!*"

That Sunday night me and the rest of the Krew chilled at Mr. B's masonry yard. We had two Swisher Sweets and a forty of malt wrapped in brown paper that we passed around. And there was also some kind of pink-colored wine too. I'd tell you who hooked up the Sweets and drinks, but I promised I'd keep it on the low. Let's just say if you asked King Tut nice and threw in a extra dollar or two, he might be able to facilitate things. Trick's little sister, Lakisha, told me how *facilitate* basically means where someone makes something happen. But about King Tut and whatnot, you didn't hear it from me.

One part of my face was still a little black and blue from the campsite beatdown. I sipped from the forty and listened to Big Vance. "Come on, Kid. Warren's bro slings sizzurp on Magnolia. You know Magno's pieced up, posted up, and ready to mash."

I asked, "How you know that?"

Vance was all, "How many slangers you met who ain't?"

I sort of cheated with my answer. "Wes. Over at Jefferson." Wes was the guy who used to hook up my liquid bars. I hadn't got my lean on since we started training for the H-Town Throw Down, and I felt way better that way. But as far as I knew Wes never had a gun his own self. Even if his junior partner Latrell did that one time.

Vance shook his head. "That's when he's at school, son. He for damn sure pack after hours."

I let the Krew know, "I ain't trying to get shot or shackled."

Trick shook his head. "Tell me this ain't about New York."

I put it down like, "So what if it is? What if *you* had a ticket out? Trick? Vance? I don't even gotta ask you, Ru."

Ru stuck his three middle fingers up in my grill. "Read between the lines, Kid."

Big Vance shook his head. "New York or no New York, the vote's three to one, Kid."

Ru piped up. "When do we do this, T?"

Trick looked over at me. "Maybe Kid's right. Maybe we roll to Magnolia tonight. No guns. No chains. No knives. Just hand to hand. And toe to toe."

Vance threw down, "Hell nah. We already decided. Right here, same time tomorrow. Seven o'clock. Then we roll to the spot, take care of biz-nass."

I stood up. "I ain't down. Plus, that's when the train's rolling out. Let's do it tonight. Like how Trick said."

Vance just pretended I wasn't there and asked Ru, "You one hundred your moms still keeps the Beretta in the freezer?"

Ru was all, "Shyeah. One hundred, mane."

Vance sipped the forty and kept pressing. "Foshizzle fo sure?"

Ru whipped his moms's Beretta from out of his back pocket and everyone leaned back. Even Vance. It was a real small pistol with a wood-grain handle.

Vance got 'gized. "Damn, Ru! And you got lead?"

Ru motioned to the forty in V's hand. "Toss that."

V tossed the forty bottle a good ten feet. Onto the

dirt. Ru fired a round at the bottle. But the bullet went real wide.

Trick got up in Ru's grill. "This my daddy's spot. Do I gotta beat your ass silly?"

I got up and stood over my bike. "I'm out. And tomorrow you ain't gonna find me on Magno turf. If y'all knew anything, you'd know we already done beat them."

The Krew scoped me hard. Vance was first to talk. "Easy for you to say, Mr. New York."

Then it was Ru's turn. "Yo, Kid. I know you ain't tryin' to hear me, but they gonna eat you up, spit you out, and ship you home UPS ground rate. Guess you wanna be knowed as the fairy in the background of some G-La video for the rest of your life."

I told him, "Hey, Ru, I know Cali didn't work out. That don't mean NYC ain't gonna do right by me."

Trick shook his head. "Know what I don't get? Soon as you rep B-town, you wanna leave it."

I set Trick straight. "Going to NYC don't mean I forget where I'm from. It's my shot to take B-town worldwide. Can't you get that?"

Trick looked away from me. "Yeah. Whatever. Don't think when you drag ass back that you still part of the Krew just 'cause that's how it went for Ru." Trick fronting all hard like that made me bite my lip till I tasted blood again.

Big V had to chime in. "You know Magno's mad posted up. You ain't a partner, partner. You punk, punk."

I flipped him the bird. "Fuck you, Vance."

Vance laughed like somebody'd told a gag. "Hope you know. Only reason they want you's 'cause you're albino."

Vance saying that was the pot calling the kettle black, and I told him so. "Yeah? You're white, and they don't want you."

Vance's forehead was set to pop a vein. He asked, "What telegram you trying to deliver, pickle licker?"

I told him, "You figure it out, fatty-no-moves."

Vance went for the Beretta in Ru's right hand. But Ru yanked the pistol back, out of his reach. V got up and started to wrestle around with Ru. "Gimme that." V snatched the gun away from him and pointed it at my stomach.

I stood my ground. "What? You really wanna shoot me, V? Go ahead! Come on!"

Me and V locked eyes. After a short second Vance looked at the ground. I got on my bike and rolled off. I didn't hear a peep out of anyone in the Krew. But I could feel them watching me roll. It wasn't but a minute later and

I heard someone bust a cap in the distance. Unless maybe it was that old Camaro backfiring its way around B-town.

It was my last night in my bedroom. I couldn't really sleep. Even with that forty making me kind of tired, I still couldn't drift all the way off. But finally I got halfway there. You know that feeling like when you step down off a curb, but then you look around and you're just in bed. 'Cept my eyes stayed closed and I was still dozing. All these pictures flashed in my head and I couldn't move my body. All I could do was watch the pictures pop on my eyelids. I saw me ride my bike past the refineries at night. Next I saw me and Earl work inside a refinery. Both me and Earl had so much grease all over our faces we looked like them old-time movies where Anglos put grease on to front like they're black.

Then I was on my bike. Pedaling my best to beat out a train to a road crossing. No matter how hard I pedaled I couldn't get going fast enough. Looked for sure like I wasn't gonna beat it. I felt hands on my shoulders. It was Alicia on back of my bike. Then she fell off and I started going faster. I just barely beat the train to the crossing. I waited for it to pass. I hoped Alicia would be on the other side after it did. But she was gone.

Next in the dream, me and the Krew were in the Magnolia section of Beaumont. All of us had gats. We shot at the windows of the apartment complex where Magno Clique was. And they shot back. I felt Alicia's hands on my shoulders again. I woke up. "Huh! Who's there?"

Someone was all, "Shhh . . ."

My desk lamp flicked on. I sat up and squinted. When my eyes could see it was Lori, she stumbled over. She sat down on my bed but almost slipped off it. You could tell she'd been sippin'. Bigtime. She wore a little pink lady's underwear thing. The kind you see in the Sears catalogue. But it showed even more skin than them kinds.

Real tender and nice, she put her hand through my hair and asked me, "You know I'm proud of you, right? Hey, who's got beer breath in here?"

"So what? *You* been sippin' codeine again."

"Ever tried it?"

I told her straight up, "Last time I tried it's the last time I'm ever trying it."

"What do you say we stop pretending. Okay, Kid?"

"Pretend about what?"

"For one thing, let's not pretend you don't know about me and Earl."

"I ain't telling."

"That's not what I mean."

"Dad wouldn't have no love for me telling."

Lori leaned over me real slow. I thought she was gonna

kiss me on the lips. But she just kissed me on the forehead. "You haven't ever touched a woman, have you, Breslin?"

She took my hand and put it on her left tit. I didn't even know where it was till after it was already there. It was warm and smooth. I yanked my hand away quick as I could. "I ain't trying to touch you there."

She went back to putting her hand through my hair. "Shhhh . . ."

I folded my arms across my chest and told her straight up, "I ain't doing nothing with you. And I already got me a lady."

"You're virgin as Mary, ain't you?" I couldn't even look at her after she said that. She stroked me on the neck. "It's no big deal, sweetie. Everyone starts out that way."

"Not me. I been with lotsa boppers before."

She laughed. Like she knew I was lying and she enjoyed catching me out. "Oh, I'm sorry. As in who, for instance?"

"Why can't you just act like a . . . like a regular person?"

Her voice got lower. "Why can't you?" She took my hand and put it over her waist and down toward her . . . you know.

But when she leaned in to kiss me I jumped up from

the bed. I yelled at her, "You better leave or I'ma tell Earl, and Dad too!"

She looked like I'd smacked her. "New York ain't gonna make a lick of difference. You'll always be a loser, Breslin. Just like your daddy." She stumbled and slinked off and slammed the door on her way out. For a second it felt just like the week before. That maybe the Throw Down and everything had only been a dream.

That morning, when I walked into Larson's Pawn, the bells on his door jingled that same way again. Like the way you hear in old-time Christmas songs. Mr. Larson was scoping the *Beaumont Enterprise*. He checked me out over his half-lens glasses rims. "Looky here."

I pulled out a hundred-dollar bill. He was all, "Too bad I just unloaded that ring."

"But you said . . ."

"Ahh, I got ya." Mr. Larson chuckled it up. He shuffled around and found the ring. "Thirty-seven-fifty."

I slid the hundred-dollar bill over the counter. Mr. Larson took the paper and held it up to the light. I told him, "Fifty back's good."

He shook his head. "Thirty-seven-fifty. That's sixty-two-fifty back. Count it." He slid the ring and all my change over to me. I picked up the paper and change bit by bit. It was all there.

"Thanks, Mr. Larson."

"Folks call me Wolf."

"That's your real name?"

"Real as real gets." He made a gag howl but it sounded a lot like a real wolf does.

I grabbed up the ring. "Speaking of real, how much to put a real one in here?"

Mr. Larson shook his head. "Real ice? Boy your age shouldn't stress about diamonds and such."

"How much?"

"Mmm, it's over a carat. You're talking three K minimum for that size rock."

"That ain't so bad."

"Okay, Rockefeller."

"I'm going to New York today, Mr. Larson."

"Good for you."

I started to walk away but he called me back. "Son. If you're serious about getting a real stone, check out the diamond district in that big city."

"Where?"

"Forty-eighth to Forty-sixth streets, 'tween Fifth and Sixth avenues."

I repeated the address since I remember better when I do that. "Diamond district?" I asked. "You been up to New York?"

"Mmm-hmm. You want the real deal, go to the source. That goes for everything in this life."

"What's the best place in the district?"

"No difference. Only one thing you gotta know. The higher the floor, the better the diamonds."

"All the way to the top, then, Mr. Larson."

Mr. Larson must have liked that 'cause he shook his head and laughed. Just before I opened the door I saw the gun case with all the pistols in it. The one with the red-tape handle was gone. "Lemme ask you one more thing."

Wolf shook his head. "You gotta be eighteen to even look at those."

"Who said I ain't? Anyway, it's not that."

"Then what is it?"

"What would you do if your best friend asked you to do something you didn't want to do but that you're supposed to do as a friend?"

"How bad's the thing and how good's the friend?" He scoped my face. "Aww, hell. That look on your face. It ain't even a question for Wolf to answer, is it?"

My head shook slow-like without me even meaning it to. "No, sir. Rightly, I guess it ain't."

I rolled my bike through the sector of the hood where King Tut was always professional chilling. I scoped him trying to mack on a pro. I snuck up real quiet-like behind them and told her, "Your brother better step his game up."

She got throwed. "He ain't my brother."

I nodded. "He still gotta step his game up." I kept rolling past but I heard her ask Tut, "What's he talking 'bout?" I turned and saw him shake his head and grin. Got him back pretty good with that gag.

When I banked the corner I saw three girls from Jefferson. Their clothes showed so much skin I barely recognized they were from school.

"Yo, Kid. I heard about the Throw Down. The Krush Krew's dope!"

I hollered back, "Yo, thanks, Jonika."

I felt good the word was out. It made me wonder who'd put the news through the grapevine. Seemed that gossip always worked overtime. Like a team of pro street promoters. All I knew for sure was it felt good that people knew 'bout me and the Krew doing something. Something worthy. Not that we were in the newspaper or whatever, but almost like that. Maybe better than that.

Alicia skipped class with me. We chilled in her room. Mrs. Guerrero was at work. All I could think on was catching the Sunset Limited rolling East that night. I still hadn't said goodbye to no one. Alicia wanted to go with me to the depot. But she didn't have a slab. We were together on her bed. She held her stuffed coyote in her arms like it was a baby. She was half crying, really more like she had the sniffles.

I tried to touch her but she moved away. "It's only ninety days up front. After they re-sign me I'ma buy you a ticket out there to be with me."

Her eyes were all full of water, but she smiled. I kissed her and threw the stuffed coyote to the ground and just kept on kissing her.

"Alicia?"

"Hmm?"

"I'm glad you my girl, and that you made the Throw Down."

"Me too."

She turned over, then started taking off her shirt. I watched real close since it was the first time I seen her do that. Next she even took off her jeans and panties. She looked right at me and she wasn't even scared. "Okay. I'm ready."

I was a little stressed. "Ready?"

"Chill. I told you, *Mami's* at the hospital till five. And you're not in training no more either, Mr. Boxer."

I didn't know what to say. Or do.

"What's wrong? Your thing's all big. Don't you want to, with me?"

"Yeah . . . but I . . . I gave your moms my word."

"Kid. Come on. It's my first time too."

That got me real steamed. "Who said it's my first time?"

She kind of scooched back from me a little. "It isn't?"

"I had lotsa boppers, like in junior high." She turned away so I couldn't even see her face. I pulled on her shoulder but she was strong and wouldn't budge. "Alicia? I didn't really. Alicia? Just 'cause I never done it you don't gotta rub it in my face."

No matter how I touched her back she wouldn't turn back around. I didn't know what to say or do next. I looked away and saw the greenest longleaf pine growing just outside her window. Sometimes you notice stuff like that at funny times. I asked her, "That tree outside your window's a longleaf pine."

She turned and smiled. She touched me all over my face. "I think it's sexy that it's your *primero* time."

"Really? That feels good."

"*Béseme.*"

I knew what that word meant. But I was thinking too much about New York to think about kissing. "Alicia . . . when I go to New York, I wanna battle my way up. All the way to the top. You think I can?"

"I *know* you can, *bebé.*"

Then I asked her, "Would you be steamed if I thought of you like the biggest prize in the world?"

She looked confused. "What do you mean?"

"I mean, what if we waited and I only get to be with you after I make it? All the way to the top."

"I don't get it."

"I want the best for you. No phony stuff. Only real stuff. No BS, never."

"What do you mean?"

"Like, you know, fake stuff. I don't want you to have that. Like if you want a coyote I'll get you a real one so you don't need a stuffed one."

"Sometimes you talk funny, Kid."

"Yeah, sometimes I feel funny. Yo, I was just thinking, if I stack enough paper, then you don't gotta be under your moms's roof anymore."

"Shut up about her, okay?"

"Okay. Leesha?"

"What?"

"You know what you been saying 'bout the Krew and all?"

"Sorry 'bout that."

"No, I been thinking. It's funny. All I used to think about was me and the Krew being the first b-boys to put B-town on the map. Now that we done that together, I'm leaving B-town behind. By myself." I partly felt proud about what me and the Krew had done. Another part of me felt bad 'cause the Krew felt bad. It was hard to straight out say all that, even to Leesha. But the thing about her was you didn't have to spell everything out. She got it anyway.

"Maybe you should stay, B."

"I don't know, Leesha. I never got a break like this. A chance to get paid and make the Kid B name shine."

She looked sad. "I get it."

She kissed me hard and I kissed her back nice.

She pulled away and gave me that little Alicia smile. She whispered, "Forget your word." First we just mugged down and held each other tight. What went down next I'm not gonna talk about—but you get what I'm saying.

It was still the same ol' Monday, but I left Alicia feeling like the day was different. Like everything had changed and was more alive. But a little part of me felt like it had been lost. I figured she must of felt that way too. Maybe even more than me. I rolled through her neighborhood and banked onto the street that lines up with the train tracks. I saw Trick stone chillin' by hisself. Quiet. I slowed and stopped. I couldn't figure what it did. Trick nodded to me. "Saw you rolling to Leesha's 'bout a hour back. Get you some honey love?"

I rolled up my shoulders. I knew Trick didn't want to chatter 'bout Leesha. At least I knew I didn't. "What it do, T? Word's already on the street 'bout what the Krew did in H-town."

T looked at the ground. "I'm scared."

" 'Bout the Clique?"

Trick nodded. "Damont heard it through the g-vine—Magno's posted up like a fence." I knew he was right. They'd for sure be on the lookout for the Krew and probably had knives and maybe even heat.

I shook my head. "You shouldn't go."

"One more soldier's one more soldier."

"Ain't none of us soldiers, T. Tell the Krew to call it off. I got a real bad feeling 'bout it."

"I got that same bad feeling, Kid. The diff is, I'm gonna be there for the Krew. You ain't."

I looked at the ground.

Trick patted me. "Yo, Kid. If, no, *when* you make the bigs, don't forget who you came up with."

Sad as the whole thing was, I scoped Trick and grinned. "Already."

I rolled out to my crib. 'Bout the only things I took from out my room was all my posters. I didn't have one of them cardboard things you're supposed to put posters in. So I folded them up and put them in the little green backpack my moms bought me back in second grade. I looked into Dad's room. He was passed out with a bottle of scotch. I sat down on the bed and it didn't bother his sleeping none. I just looked at him and wished he had maybe been around a little more and spent more time kicking it with me. Not just being on the road and drinking whiskey. Or fixing junk on the truck with Earl and stuff.

I went outside to bungee cord the green backpack to my bike. On the porch Lori smoked on the nicest chair. She didn't even look up. There was nothing to say. But she chimed over to me, "So, the big superstar's all grown up."

"I ain't talking to you."

"You just did. Besides, who else you gonna talk to around here?"

"I got stuff to do. Say goodbye to him."

Lori took a long drag. "Sure, whatever. Too bad for you he's taking one of his naps."

"Yeah, too bad for everybody. 'Specially him." I walked over the porch and back into the house. I turned back around and scoped Lori through the screen. "Why you marry him to start with?"

She looked at the porch floor. "It was pretty much him or nobody."

"That's sad. I mean—I didn't mean it like that."

"I don't care how you meant it."

I told her, "Yeah, me neither."

Lori flicked her smoke butt onto the porch. Then grinded it out.

I knocked on Earl's door and he opened. He flopped

231

onto his bed and grabbed a rubber ball. He kept squeez-
ing it like he was stressed and asked me, "Wow, can I have
your autograph?"

"Yeah, if you take me to the depot."

"Take a bus."

"So. That's it?"

Earl stopped messing with the rubber ball and looked
at me. "What?"

"Nothing. I just thought maybe . . . never mind."
That was all I could think to say at first, but then I did
think of something else.

"You know what, Earl?" He started bouncing the ball
off the ceiling. "Ever since Mom died, you pretty much
been the most worst older brother in history."

Earl beaned the hell out my face with the ball.

"Fuck you!" I heard myself shout. But I heard it like
someone else said it.

I slammed the door and heard Earl yell, "You'll
come crawling back. Well, don't bother, you nigger-
lovin' wannabe!"

I can't even remember opening the door back up.
I ran at Earl. My right hand smashed into the side of
his head.

"What the—" I kicked him before he could finish his

sentence. I saw him tumble backwards to the floor. Seeing that felt great. He got up and grabbed his baseball bat.
He grinned to let me know he was gonna enjoy whuppin'
me. "You're gonna catch it now."

I scrambled out his room and into the kitchen. I
opened up two drawers at once and grabbed for the
biggest knife I seen. Earl strolled into the kitchen jiggling the baseball bat. He scoped the knife and shouted,
"Drop it! Now!"

I motioned to his bat. "Nu-uh. You drop it."

Earl got all red in the face. "I'm not gonna ask
you again."

He came for me. Still jiggling the bat. Then all at once
he swung at me. I saw it coming, ducked, and came up
quick with the knife. I couldn't feel it slice into him. But
he dropped the bat. And you could see 'bout half a inch
deep into his arm meat. Earl sort of wobbled and fell to
his backside. "Oh my God! You *gashed* me! You little son
of a bitch!"

A part of me chuckled about him calling me a son of a
bitch. 'Cause we both got the same moms and all.

His eyes showed how scared he was. Like how he used
to look as a little kid just before Dad hauled off on him.
With all the blood dripping on the kitchen floor, for a

short second I felt even more scared than his bug-eyed self. But I squinted real close at his arm and you couldn't see bone. I figured the cut wasn't so bad as all that.

Earl grabbed at his bloody arm. He blubbered like a little baby. His face twisted up and his breath got funny. It went in and out faster and faster. "Why'd you hurt me? You didn't have to go and slash me." He scoped my face like I was *his* big brother or somebody. Then a purple vein popped on his forehead. He shouted, "You think you're the shit? You're nothing. Nothing!"

Dad shuffled into the kitchen half awake and full on drunk. He saw Earl bleeding on the floor. "What the hell's going on?" Earl just kept blubbering. And I didn't know what to say. Lori poked her head into the kitchen and let out a scream. I pushed past her and Dad stepped in front of me. He was too drunk to really look at me straight. "Where you think you're going?"

"To say goodbye to my real moms."

I hoofed it past him and out the front door right quick. I jumped on my bike. But fast as I pedaled, I couldn't get away from the picture of Earl's twisted-up face.

BREAKBEAT 17
CLEAR THE VICINITY

Lamar Cemetery's where they kept Moms's body ever since she died. I figured I'd be in New York for a long stretch so I should say goodbye. But with the Sunset Limited rolling out at 8:14, I didn't even have the chance to pick dandelions, let alone wildflowers. I took a shortcut past one of the oil refineries. The puffs of smoke it made were the only clouds against a pure blue sky. But no one could count the puffs coming out the smokestacks for true clouds. When I really scoped around I did spot one little baby cloud way out East. All by itself. Usually clouds are like trees and people and if you see one hanging around you'll spot a few more.

When I got to the little cemetery I locked my bike up to the front gate, even though I was the only person there.

I liked how the grass was fresh cut. And not chock-full of long weeds like back in the neighborhood. I saw red flowers on one of the graves. Next to the flowers was a little rebel flag. It surprised me 'cause the grave didn't look old enough to be from way back then.

It didn't take long to get to where I was going. I got on my knees in front of her grave. I touched the stone and it was cold. Awful cold. The dried old purple flowers there on the grave felt warmer. There was a lot of things I was confused about. Trick. The whole Krew. Alicia. New York. Dad. Lori. Earl. I read the gravestone out loud to myself. Like it wasn't already knowed by heart. GERALDINE KIRWIN—LOVING WIFE AND MOTHER. I wished she was still alive, even just to talk to for a day or a minute.

A car sat on its horn and I stood up. I looked across the little cemetery. I saw Dad's pickup parked just outside the fence. I looked one last time at the stone.

I made for the pickup and heard the engine running. Across the way from the cemetery was a skeezy bar with red neon flashing its name, ENUS V's. I could tell Dad was still off his head and shouldn't of been driving.

I got close and he told me, "Get in." I did.

"You ain't gonna whup me?"

"It's been a long minute since we spent any time, just

you and me." He looked out over the cemetery and shook his head. "Never could stand walking over a bunch of dead and rotted buried folks. Not even at your age."

He grabbed between his legs and yanked up a Lone Star tallboy from a twelve-pack box. "Have your first beer with me." He cracked it open and handed it to me. It was icy cold.

I told him straight up, "I've drank beer before."

"Not with me you haven't." He cracked one open for hisself and sipped. Dad looked more tired and bothered and beat down by life and things than I ever seen him. He scoped the red neon sign down the block that kept flashing the name ENUS V's.

I sipped my beer and asked him if Earl would be all right. Dad let out a little beer burp and nodded.

I took another sip. "Tell him . . . tell him I'm sorry."

Dad wouldn't look at me. Like maybe he was trying to hide from me seeing him 'bout to cry or something. His voice came out heavy and thick. "You know, I always had the feeling you thought I drove her to it." He went from hiding his face to looking right at me with that blue laser stare he's got.

"Yeah. I think I did used to think that."

"I don't know. Maybe you were right. I'll tell you one

thing, Kid. Your mother sure as hell wasn't perfect. But she had, she *has*, no equal."

"After Moms, I never got how you could be with . . . Look. I gotta tell you something 'bout Earl . . ."

"What about him, Kid?"

"And Lori."

"I'm listening."

"Well, it's about Earl and Lori. Like, doing things together and stuff. When you're driving."

Dad shook his head. "You think I wanna hear your clack about them carrying on?"

"She told you?"

"Didn't have to. Suppose I should get all riled up, kick both their sorry asses out of my house. Sad thing is, I really don't care at this point."

"I think you should." I was even more surprised than Dad that it came out of my mouth.

But Dad didn't get too steamed. "I think you should keep your two bits to yourself, Kid." He pointed over to Enus V's. "You know, that's where I met your mother. Twenty-three years, two months ago."

I scoped the nasty joint out one last time. Then I patted Dad on the shoulder and kept my hand there. I could see me having my hand on his shoulder made him feel funny. So I pulled it away. He asked, "When's that train pulling out?"

"Eight-fourteen."

Dad peeped a glance at his old Elgin Durabalance. It said 7:34. Dad told me and Earl once that he bought the watch after he kept being late for dates with Mom. She'd told him if he was late one more time it would be the last time. Kind of like Dap at the refinery 'cept between a woman and man instead of a boss and worker. Anyway, he told me and Earl that's why he'd bought it. Dad might've muffed up a lot of things. But he was never late for anything as long as I could remember. "Let's get a-ramblin'. My boy's got big things to do in the big city."

Off to the West you could hear two sets of police sirens getting closer and closer. I had to check on the Krew. I told Dad, "I gotta roll by a spot off Magnolia right quick." Magnolia was only five minutes from the cemetery.

Dad asked, "Why?"

"I can't tell you just now." We put my bike and backpack in the pickup bed and rolled toward Magnolia. Some old country song played through the static of the truck radio. Dad lit up a smoke and sipped from the Lone

Star between puffs. The sirens got more and more loud. I asked, "Can I ask you something?" Which I guess is already asking something.

"What's on your mind?"

"Who was your best friend in high school?"

"That would have been Randy, I suppose. The two of us sure as hell chased our share of skirts. That was before your mother."

"What was the most worst thing you ever did to Randy?"

"Why do you ask?"

"No reason. Are y'all still best friends?"

It took him a long minute to answer. "I don't know that fellas our age got best friends."

The Magnolia section's even more beat up than my hood or Alicia's. We were almost there. I thought I could hear a ambulance siren or two mixing in with the police sirens. We rolled past a boarded-up building that said MAGNOLIA SOCIAL CLUB. A smaller sign on the tumbledown building said WHERE GROWN FOLKS COME TO PARTY. Three mean-looking dudes in their thirties and maybe forties stared when we rolled past.

Dad shook his head. "See that? They don't even respect their own property."

I was gonna say something 'bout Mr. Bilcox and stuff. Instead I asked, "When's the last time someone painted *our* house?"

Dad got steamed for a short second. Then he flashed that big grin of his and was all, "Too bad you've got a train to catch, 'cause boy do I got a job in mind for you."

I pointed to the right. "Down there."

He turned to the right. "Where the hell am I taking you?"

"I already explained how I can't explain it right now."

"Christ, Kid. It's quarter till. That train pulls out in half an hour." I told you how he's always too early to be late.

"Over there." I showed him the complex where Warren and his cousin Branford lived. Branford's the guy who I told you slangs sizzurp. Six police cruisers and two ambulances were already parked outside. The police were shooing away a mess of rubberneckers from the neighborhood. Before the truck had even come to a stop I jumped out my door. I told Dad, "Stay here. I'll be right back."

I ran into the mix and heard Dad yell, "Kid! Get your ass back here! Now!" The crowd seemed like they were jonesing to see someone hurt. Not like the crowd in the

rec center who wanted to scope people showcasing something they were good at. A big police guy had the Beretta
in one plastic bag and the red-taped snubnose in another.

A real peewee police officer stood in front of me. He
tried to block my view. But he was too short. "Police
scene. Clear the area." He jiggled his nightstick around
the way Earl had jiggled his bat. I ignored him and scoped
over his head to Vance, Ruina, Warren, and Izzle. They
were all face-down on the pavement. And all four of them
were handcuffed behind the back. Then I saw a stretcher
coming out the apartment with Peanut on it. The front of
his white tee was stained blood red. He looked graveyard
dead but I wasn't for sure.

I shouted to Vance and Ruina, "Where's Trick?"

Vance, Ruina, Izzle, and Warren all scoped me from
their places on the ground. Ruina yelled, "Peanut
capped him."

Big Vance shouted at me, "You shoulda been here,
faggot!" A police guy pretended like he was about to kick
Vance in the face. And he told Vance to shut up.

I scoped Trick being lugged to a ambulance on a
stretcher. One of them chalk blue uniform ambulance
guys held the front of the stretcher. The other one had
the back. There were no police by Trick's ambulance so I

was able to get real close. Trick looked dog tired. Like he needed to sleep two days straight. I looked at my feet. "Vance is right. I shoulda been here."

Trick's words came out slow. "Naw, Kid. It was three wrongs to one right."

One of the chalk blue uniform guys moved Trick's muffed-up shoulder. Tired as he looked, Trick yelled out real loud. I put my hand on T's leg. "Yo, T. I'm X times a factor of two for sure you gonna be back to new in no time flat."

Trick shook his head real slow. "Come on, Kid. Every lamebrain knows there's no such thing as two hundred percent."

Somebody jammed a stick into my back. I turned. It was the peewee police guy who'd got in my face before. "All right, visitation's over. Clear the vicinity." I saw water in Trick's eyes, just before the chalk blue uniform guy slammed the back ambulance door shut.

I felt some water coming on too. But I didn't want nobody there to see. So I held it back. The peewee police guy got in my grill. "Push off."

I backed up toward Dad's pickup and heard Ru yell out from the ground. "Hey! Mess New York up. But don't let it mess you up."

Then Vance shouted out from the deck, "Don't never come back to B-town, punk!" But the way V said it you knew he was more sad than mad about things.

Two police guys lifted Warren off the deck. They hustled him over to a police car and yanked open the back door. I turned and made for the pickup. Some of the crowd chuckled at Warren like the whole thing was a gag. Even if they were supposed to be his neighbors. I heard Warren yell out, "Yo, B!"

I spun around. Warren looked at me, calm and direct. The two police guys tried to push him into the back of the police car. But Warren stood hard so he could say what he wanted to say. And the way he said it I knew he meant it. "Grind and shine, Kid. Grind and shine."

THE SUNSET LIMITED

Dad was the only person on the train platform. He stood rock still. Only moving his left hand to puff on his cigarette now and again. The train window had a metal frame that almost made it look like Dad was in a picture. Like I wasn't seeing him right there and then, but sometime frozen in the past. How it is with pictures. The train gave a jolt and started forward. The picture in the frame of the train window started to move and Dad put his right hand up. It wasn't really a wave. More like his hand reaching out to catch a ball fitting to fly overhead or something. I put my right hand on the window and held on to the picture of him shining through the glass. And I remembered how he held me up in that picture in the orange shoebox in the closet. The train kept moving East and the picture of him on the platform kept moving West. Till it passed by and out of view completely.